Detonator

A Dave Haggard Thriller

By

Larry Matthews

W & B Publishers

USA

W & B Publishers

For information:
W & B Publishers
Post Office Box 193
Colfax, NC 27235
www.a-argusbooks.com

ISBN: 978-0-6922859-2-3
ISBN: 0-69222859-2-X

Book Cover designed by Dubya

Printed in the United States of America

Thank You

This is a work of fiction. It is a made-up story and any connection to persons living or dead is purely coincidental.

There are four exceptions and I would like to thank them for graciously making cameos in Detonator.

First, Johnny Holliday, the legendary Washington-area broadcaster. Johnny and I have been friends for over forty years.

Charlie Steiner, the play-by-play man behind Vin Scully for the Los Angeles Dodgers. Charlie and I have known each other for decades.

Dave McConnell, the larger-than-life Capitol Hill reporter for WTOP, Washington's top-rated all-news station. Dave and I have sat through many boring Congressional hearings.

And, finally, Wendy Rieger, one of the anchors on NBC4, Washington's top-rated television news department. Wendy is smart, gorgeous, and a hell of a reporter.

I am grateful that you all agreed to make appearances in this book.

Washington, D.C.
A warm September night

Forty thousand people sat on the bomb, cheering and swilling beer, eating hot dogs, and watching the batter. First place was on the line for both teams, Washington in the East and Los Angeles in the West. The crowd roared with every pitch. The air was thick with sweat and humidity and the heat that lingers into fall in the Nation's Capital.

A team of F.B.I. agents was coming through the gates, running and following a tall, thin agent who believed she could pick the man out of the crowd. She knew she would get one chance, one shot—if she beat the odds. If not, the conflagration would be unimaginable.

Charlie Steiner was in the visitor's booth at Nationals Park, calling the game for L.A.

"Bottom of the ninth, game tied at five." He wiped his face with a towel, uncomfortable in the Washington heat and humidity. "Swing and a miss."

Across the field, in a standing room area where most of the fans had downed one beer for each inning, the crowd was noisy and some of them were making out with strangers, not paying attention to what was happening on the field. One man was paying very close attention. He was a dark-skin man wearing a Washington baseball cap.

He carried an out-of-state driver's license that identified him as a man named Gutierrez, but that was not his name. He was a Pakistani, a member of the terrorist group known as The Knife, and he was watching the batter.

In his pocket was a wireless detonator. He was waiting to see if the batter hit a home run, which would set off fireworks at the park. The fireworks would be greater than anyone knew.

They are swine, these people. They breed like rabbits and they spread their death and shamelessness into our very homes. What will happen tonight will make what has happened to them in the past seem like a walk in the park. It is for glory that I have come to this moment.

The next pitch was right down the middle, low and into sweet spot on the bat that sent the ball soaring into the night sky.

The man, the crowd, and the F.B.I. agents stopped to watch it as it rose into the lights.

Chapter One

Ikram Ali Ghazali hurried through Union Station and out onto Massachusetts Avenue into the light rain that made the summer heat steamy and close. To him, it felt like Pakistan without the smells and beggars. He had come to the place of Satan to die and find Paradise. He had no time for sentimentality but he allowed himself a memory of the food stalls that had scented the neighborhood where he had attended the madrasa, learned to hate the West, and memorized every word of the Qur'an. He paused and recalled the first words of Al-Fatihah, The Opener: 1) *In the name of Allah Most Gracious Most Merciful.* 2) *Praise be to Allah the Cherisher and Sustainer of the Worlds.*

This man's heart was not most merciful. He seethed with a desire to watch his enemies suffer. He looked around and saw himself in the heart of the beast. He recalled the orders of his master, "Present a passive face to those around you and, when noticed, smile and appear docile. Strike with the venom of a snake."

The tourist bus was waiting in the circle outside the station and he could see the dome of the United States Capitol as he ran to join the line of other tourists, none of whom spoke English. The driver was a dark-skin man like himself, with straight black hair. The group had offered the cover of a tourist visit to the United States, arranged by an agency known for transporting Mexicans willing to spend money north of the border. Such tourists were always welcome in Washington.

"Prisa. Boleto por favor*" Hurry. Ticket please.* The driver looked past Ghazali at the next tourist in line. Ghazali was carrying a passport that identified him as a Mexican national named Juan Fernando Gutierrez of Mexico City.

He gave the man his ticket and climbed aboard, finding a seat next to a fat, middle-age woman.

"Es emocionante estar aquí." *It is exciting to be here.* She looked at the Capitol and smiled. "¿Es hermoso, no?" *It is beautiful, no?"*

"Si." He smiled with her. It was exciting, to be sure, after the years of study and planning. He had learned Spanish and had spent months in Central America, travelling and talking to anyone who would engage him, wringing the last of his accent out of his speech. He could speak high Spanish or low, Sonora or Oaxaca. He spoke English with a Mexican accent.

His trainer and master had told him about life in the West. "Mexicans are common and accepted, in their own way, in America. Pakistanis are suspect. In many ways, we look alike to the whites and blacks in places like Washington or New York City. And a man travelling on a Pakistani passport will be watched. A Mexican would be welcomed, so long as he goes home on time. A well-dressed Mexican will not be singled out at a concert at the Kennedy Center. A poorly dressed Mexican will not be noticed at a construction site. It is all about appearances." By the time anyone noticed the man who called himself Gutierrez, it would be too late.

He had become an expert on electric grids and he had come to America to turn out the lights. *It will be a tribute to the martyrs when these dogs live in darkness,* he thought. *Let them live in caves and we will see how they survive.* The grid in America was like a child waiting to be taken in the night. *These people are fools.*

The bus drove past the usual tourist spots and stopped at a few like the Washington Monument, the Lincoln Memorial, and Pentagon, where it idled in a large parking lot while the tourist guide explained that it was the largest office building in the world and headquarters of the most powerful military the world has ever known.

The man who called himself Gutierrez nodded in admiration and resentment. *You lock the front door but leave the back door open. I have come to visit.*

He had no further use of the group. He told the driver he had business to attend to and would rejoin his fellow travelers in a day or two. He got off the bus at 14th Street and Pennsylvania Avenue, not bothering to collect his luggage in the storage bin beneath the passenger compartment. He carried a backpack that contained what he needed. He checked into the Willard, went to his room, and studied the documents in his backpack. They contained the names of the Homeland Security employees who were tasked with protecting the American electric grid. All of them had the highest security clearances. Obtaining their information had been easy. Obtaining the weakness in the grid had been even easier.

He opened his laptop and logged into a program that provided him with the web identity of a man in Arizona who had no knowledge of Juan Gutierrez or his mission. A software program he had been provided put Gutierrez anywhere he chose. Once in, he opened a program that exposed the grid in the Washington area.

" Bismi-llāhi r-raḥmāni r-raḥīm." *In the name of Allah, Most Gracious, Most Merciful*. His voice was a whisper. He slid his finger over the touch pad and watched the curser slide to the point he had selected and, with a left click, he turned out the lights in North Arlington. *I am here. I have sent you a message.*

***

"Oh, crap!" Dave Haggard threw up his hands as others around him moaned and complained about the outage. "How long until the generator kicks in?" He was in the Now News newsroom in Rosslyn, across the Potomac River from Georgetown. It was his first day back. He was hung over from a summer of self-pity basted in Tennessee whiskey. His stomach was giving consideration to projectile vomit. When the lights came back on they would reveal a pasty thirty-something who looked like hell.

"One minute," came the reply from someone Dave could not see. "But it's about five minutes before everything boots up again."

"Goddam it! You'd think that if we can put a man on the moon we could keep the lights on." Sid Slackey ran Now News from a small office where his rants and ass-chewings could be heard—and often seen—by the staff.

His office had no windows and he now sat in the dark, smacking his desk top.

"That was a long time ago, Sid." A man named Gabriel was running the desk and had been working the phones and checking the wires on his computer screen when the lights went out. "Nobody goes to the moon anymore."

"That's the problem with this country, we don't do anything anymore." Sid was sliding into one of his "moods" and Gabriel was pushing it along.

Dave was spending the day back in the city after a summer-long recuperation from a gunshot wound he had suffered in Tennessee at the hands of a professional killer, who was now dead. News stories, no matter how important at the time, have a short shelf life and the one that had produced his wound was barely remembered, even in the news business.

"I'm bored, Sid," Dave said into the dark room. Now News had rented him and his significant other, a beauty named Elena, a condo on the beach in Ocean City, Maryland. "I hate the ocean, I hate the beach life and I hate seafood." He was trying to log on to a workstation when the power went out. "Sid, when can I come back to work?"

"When Elena says you're ready." Sid and Elena had formed a kind of alliance after Dave was shot, a pseudo-familial arrangement where Sid would play the father role to whatever role Elena chose; sister, mother, lover. "Maybe you need to dry out."

"She's not my keeper, Sid." They were yelling back and forth in the dark as the rest of the staff hoped they would shut up.

"We'll set up a test. I'll get a fire truck to speed by and you chase it. If you can run for forty blocks you can come back."

"I couldn't do that when I was in shape."

"Not my problem."

"Then I'll just sit here until I can hit the streets. I can't stand the beach another day. I need to smell some diesel and hear a Somali cab driver complain about immigrants."

The lights came on and a small cheer went up in the newsroom as the computers slowly came to life.

***

The man who called himself Gutierrez smiled and moved the curser on his laptop. The lights of Georgetown went dark. *Soon, you will all be like children screaming for your milk.*

Chapter Two

Rodell "Rod" Clark was nervous. He was sweating and his right foot was trembling as he sat watching the giant screens flash warnings about holes that were appearing in the grid. The computers were searching for the causes of the outages and the screens were alive with messages that read "searching for solution." The software that made the grid "smart" was designed to find downed wires or blown substations, not computer worms that eroded the flow of electricity. That task had been left to Clark to work out.

"Damn it!" his boss yelled. "Get this done!" It was his normal expression of problem solving.

Clark was nervous because he had made a deal with the devil, in his own assessment. He had looked at himself in the bathroom mirror one morning and decided that he just didn't care about anything anymore. Not his wife. Not his children. Not his too-large-too-expensive house. Not his pool membership. And certainly not his job. For years he had lived a life of resentment and anger. He spent his days dreaming of a life in the mountains of Montana, breathing clean air and making love to blond and freckled goddesses who, in his fantasies, populated the rural West. In his dreams he had no mortgage and no bills of any kind, just a daily joy of being alive. There were no bosses in these dreams to tell him when to come to work and when to go home. No efficiency reports.

"What the hell is going on?" He watched while his boss grew frantic as the expensive and so-called state-of-the-art smart grid software crashed and the outage cascaded throughout the Washington region. "Anybody got an explanation for this?" The man stood in front of the large monitors and shook his head. "Are we being attacked?"

Clark allowed himself a moment of happiness as he thought about the fifty-thousand dollars in twenties and hundreds he had stashed in a suitcase in a locker at the health club he despised. A matching amount would complete the deal and he would be gone, vanished, free.

"Call Homeland Security." His boss was pacing. "We're being hit. We need some big guns on this. Clark, what the hell is going on?"

"I don't know. We've got backups kicking in." Clark knew that the grid would come back to life in fifteen minutes and that this was only a warning from those who had paid him. He attempted to look concerned and frantic as he pounded his keyboard like the others in the control room, appearing to be searching for a cause and solution. Only he knew that he was the cause and the solution. It was his personal "dollars for code" program.

"It's coming back." His boss pointed at the monitors that went from red to green as the grid that provided the power that made modern life possible slowly came to life. "We need to know what happened. Clark, you're here until we get some answers."

***

The control room was three stories underground a mile off Route 7 in Loudoun County, Virginia, a distant suburb of Washington and a fast-growing high tech area of smart people who were making a killing off federal contracts, directly or indirectly.

It was located in one of the mysterious office parks that had sprouted in the region since 9/11, when Homeland Security money began to wash over the Capital area like a giant green wave. Large, plain office buildings without windows bore corporate names such as "Orzon Solutions" or "ZilTek Systems," names that meant nothing.

"SystmsSol" was the name on the building where Clark worked. An Internet search would turn up a description that was impossible to follow, just a string of fuzzy mission statements without focus. Its real purpose was to secure the nation's electric grid which, by wide agreement, was ripe for a takedown.

Clark had written the software that was designed to make the system self-healing and protected against intruders. His ardor for the project was less than his loathing for his life in the suburbs.

"Clark, my office now." His boss's "office" was a cubicle in a corner, nearly dark, illuminated only by the glow of computer screens and warning lights. "What happened?"

"It appears to be a software glitch," Clark said. "I'll work up a fix."

"And get me a report for Homeland Security. They'll want to know what happened. They're on their way, so get started." The man was humorless and officious and he had the air of someone who drank alone at night.

Clark was feeling elated in a seventh-grade kind of way; a pouty you're-gonna-be-sorry attitude that gave him the giggles. He bounced up and down in little jumps that caused the others in the control area to roll their eyes. He was known as "super geek" behind his back and his annual secret Santas always gave him plastic pocket protectors and a supply of cheap pens. He was wearing the last such gift at that moment and one of the pens bounced out and onto the floor. He didn't notice.

One of the front line supervisors leaned over to a woman at a control unit and whispered, "Guess who just got a new slide rule." She glanced at Clark and shook her head.

***

The Department of Homeland Security was created after 9/11 and scooped up other government agencies in what Americans were told was a bold attempt to make safeguarding the nation more efficient and effective. The Department's website puts it this way:

(1) In General. - The primary mission of the Department is to

(A) Prevent terrorist attacks within the United States;

(B) Reduce the vulnerability of the United States to terrorism; and

(C) Minimize the damage, and assist in the recovery, from terrorist attacks that do occur within the United States.

This broad mandate let loose the hounds within the government agencies that fell into the new Department. The hounds hunted down the untold billions of dollars that were in play in the frenzy to protect the nation. Police departments all across America, even those where the threat level is somewhere south of zero, were given grants to upgrade their equipment and install the latest surveillance gear to keep an eye out for suspicious actors. As a result, nearly every American is observed at some point in their day, whether online, on the phone, or on the highway, where police equipped with special cameras capture the license plates of passing vehicles.

All of this surveillance and spending created a problem. What to do with all of the data being collected? More billions were spent on data centers where all of this information could be stashed away. There was so much information being collected that new systems had to be devised to go through it for clues about threats. It was like looking for rain in the stratosphere. Droplets but a dearth of storms.

Another fallout from all of this was the formation of endless committees, task forces, commissions and other organizations where taxpayer money was being spent to send men and women to meetings where the topic nothing more than what the committee was doing about itself.

One such group was the Capital Area Task Force On Security, known as CATFOS. CATFOS was a collection of experts, blowhards, throwaways, shit-listees, and men and women who had fallen from favor wherever else they happened to be. The stated purpose of CATFOS was to analyze, strategize, compartmentalize, and isolate security threats to the Greater Washington Zone. In other words, it was just another government panel whose work meant, basically, nothing at all.

One of the "experts" assigned to this work was recently promoted Inspector Daniel O'Neil of the Metropolitan Police Department, the formal name of the D.C. Police. O'Neil had headed Homicide and had run afoul of official regulations in a botched investigation into the serial killer of priests. That had sent him to a dead end job at a Homeland Security backwater office where he was nearly beaten to death by a psychopathic hit man whose nickname was Brass Knuckles, now deceased. O'Neil was now recovered and enjoying a new rank in yet another backwater job, one that allowed the Police Chief to say she had assigned a high ranking D.C. Police Official to CATFOS, where, she assumed, he would vanish from all official radar.

And so it was that Inspector O'Neil found himself pulling into the parking lot at a building bearing the nonsensical name "SystmSol". He was accompanied by a tall, thin, stunningly beautiful African-American named Patricia Gant, officially an F.B.I. analyst. Unofficially, a shit-listee who had run afoul of the culture at the Hoover Building and so had been, like O'Neil, assigned to CATFOS.

Unfortunately for Rod Clark, both were experienced interrogators whose bullshit detectors were set at a very high function. O'Neil's from years on the street, Gant's from a natural talent enhanced by training at the F.B.I. Academy at Quantico.

"Let's get this over with," O'Neil said.

"Jesus, let's hope this doesn't take long. We can maybe get a decent meal in Leesburg later."

"This should be a short report. The power went out. It came back on. We can both sign it and go home."

Gant laughed and pulled out her badge as the front desk rent-a-cop looked up from a magazine. The guard's jaw dropped, a common reaction to Patricia's model-like appearance. "We're here about the power problem," she said, smirking at the man.

Chapter Three

O'Neil was a street cop. He had been through the usual training courses designed to groom the department's future leaders and give them polish and management skills. He had never lost his rough edges nor had he lost his definition of law breakers as "shit birds." He had little use for cops who spent their careers behind desks kissing the next ass up the ladder. He liked the give and take of a street encounter, where both sides know that lies and deception are in the air like balloons at a convention.

O'Neil took one look at Clark and saw an amateur bullshitter who was out of his league. The challenge was finding the bullshit and sorting it from whatever else was floating around Clark. It's not that O'Neil knew that Clark was living in a fake world. He felt it, which, in his own opinion, was the same as knowing, although a judge would require more than a cop's "feeling" about a defendant.

They were in a small, windowless conference room furnished with only a round table and four chairs. Clark was a nervous, jittery man whose eyes darted around. His legs trembled. He smiled and unsmiled the lower half of his face. He did all of this before O'Neil or Gant could say hello. Bad sign, thought O'Neil. *This guy might pee his pants before we squeeze him.*

"Hello, Mr. Clark. I'm Inspector O'Neil and this is Agent Gant." O'Neil wore what he referred to as his "Officer Friendly" face, perfectly expressed as a man who was smiling with great effort. "We're sorry to take you away from your work. We would like to get your thoughts on the outages that occurred today. We understand you wrote the security software." He gave Clark a serious, intense stare and waited for the man to crumble.

Clark's face took on several expressions at once, morphing from one to another. O'Neil had to fight the urge to laugh out loud. It looked to him like a Red Skelton routine. Then he wondered if anyone knew who Red Skelton was anymore. *They don't make comics like that anymore. Too bad.* The comic died in 1997 at an advanced age and was no longer popular at the end. O'Neil's reverie about an old television comedian had nothing to do with the interview at hand, but he was having trouble taking the interview seriously.

"I'm not sure what happened. I'll review the data and report back to you." Clark's knees were shaking.

"Do you have any evidence or even an opinion that this might have been caused by someone acting on the outside? A hacker, for instance?" Agent Gant was leaning back in her chair, looking at Clark with a casual, friendly gaze.

"Not right now, no."

"Do you think it's a possibility?"

"I don't see how. I wrote the program myself. I don't see how anyone could get inside. I wrote security elements into it. I would know and I see nothing like that. No." Clark's teeth were chattering like he had been left out in the snow, which would have been impossible given the summer heat.

"I see," O'Neil said. "So what is your working theory right now?"

"Like I said, I'll have to look at the data."

"How long will that take?"

"I don't know. A couple of days, maybe."

"That long?" Gant offered a surprised look. "Can't you just run a security program and see what comes up?"

"No, not with this. It will take more time."

O'Neil decided to swing for a home run. "Are you lying to us, Mr. Clark?"

Clark's face grew red and his eyes opened wide. He made a strangling noise. "Why would you ask me that?"

"Are you lying, Mr. Clark?" Gant's voice was soft.

Clark gasped and his chest heaved as though he couldn't breathe. "I don't know what you're talking about. Why would I lie to you?" His eyes had a frantic, animal look to them as he surveyed the room for an escape route. "I need to go to the bathroom. I think I'm going to be sick."

O'Neil stood and walked to the door, opened it, and waved Clark into the hall. He followed him to a door marked with symbols for both men and women and waited in the hall as Clark opened the door and went inside. He heard water running and the toilet flush. Minutes went by and there was no sign of Clark. O'Neil tried the door and found it locked. He pounded on the door and yelled, "Open up, Mr. Clark!" There was no response. He pounded on the door again and pushed his shoulder against it and realized that he could not break it down.

"Gant! Get building security. He's not coming out." O'Neil's hollering brought an assortment of workers into the hall and they watched, wide-eyed, as O'Neil pounded on the bathroom door.

Five minutes later a chubby man in work clothes picked through a ring of keys and unlocked the door to the bathroom. It was empty. One of the foam ceiling tiles over the toilet had been pushed aside. Clark was gone. He had used the liquid hand soap to write a message on the mirror. "Fuck you. Bye." There was a frowny face under the message.

O'Neil began to laugh. "At least it's getting interesting," he said.

Gant called her office to report a "fugitive" escape. She used her smartphone to take pictures of the mirror and the ceiling. She glared at O'Neil. "How did you let this happen?"

"Maybe you'd like to check the ceiling. He might still be up there."

"What do you want to bet that his car is gone."

"Ya think?" O'Neil made some calls of his own and was walking out the door when two Loudoun County Sheriff's deputies pulled into the parking lot, sirens blasting and lights flashing.

Chapter Four

Ikram Ali Ghazali, aka Juan Gutierez walked up Massachusetts Avenue in the sunshine, wearing what he hoped would mark him as a tourist from Mexico. He wore sandals, knee-length shorts, and an off-white guayabera shirt with four patch pockets. The shirt was worn on the outside of his shorts. He was wearing a "Washington, D.C." baseball hat purchased from a street merchant on the Mall. He had a throw-away camera and made a show of taking pictures of the embassies and other elegant buildings as he walked in a northwesterly direction, crossed Sheridan Circle, and, just past the Embassy of Japan, came to his destination.

The Islamic Center of Washington was once the largest Muslim house of worship in North America. It was built in the years after World War Two when the world was testing the idea of tolerance. It was dedicated by President Dwight Eisenhower who proclaimed, "America would fight with her whole strength for your right to have here your own church and worship according to your own conscience." Such sentiments were no longer in fashion as Ghazali approached the ornate façade of the mosque.

Ghazali harbored no brotherly feelings toward anyone in the West and very few in the Muslim world. He even hated his own name, structured in the Western manner by his father, who spent his entire life feeling inferior to people whom the son believed were nothing more than debased dogs. First. Middle. Last. He would change that if he survived.

He entered the large prayer room and knelt on one of the rugs that had been donated by Iran during the days of the Shah. He wept as he prayed. He felt cleansed when he stood and walked out onto Massachusetts Avenue and looked up toward the home of the Vice President of the United States. He smiled to himself, vowing to savor the moment when the dogs were baying at the moon and begging for their electric lights and televisions.

He walked down into Rock Creek Park and found the spot where a message was waiting for him in a grove of small trees near the creek. The message was under an artificial rock that would be identified as phony by even a casual observer, something he noted and promised to call to the attention of his handler as soon as possible.

The message was in Arabic and was encoded, so someone who came upon it by accident would have no idea what it was. He put the paper in his pocket and spent a few minutes walking in the park, appearing to be just another happy hiker on a beautiful summer day. He stopped to gaze at the flowers and the green foliage, snapping pictures and lifting his face to the sun. Several gay men who were sunning themselves on a patch of grass waved and smiled and rubbed each other's backs. Ghazali smiled back and told himself that such men would be stoned to death in a just world. *Smile and appear docile*, he told himself.

He went back to his room and deciphered the message:

Meet Clark at station number one
Use Gutierrez as your name until further notice
Watch for snakes

He was disturbed by the implications of the message. *Station number one* was a house on the Eastern Shore in the town of Cambridge. *Use Gutierrez* was a warning that he may be under surveillance and he should offer no sign of his Muslim faith until it was deemed safe. *Watch for snakes* was a warning that something had gone wrong

He was being told to rent a car, go to Cambridge, to deal with Rodell Clark, the traitor. Clark had been told he was dealing with a Mexican national who was angry with America over its drug policies and wanted nothing more than to teach America a lesson by displaying the weakness in its electric grid. *Such a simple thing. What a stupid man*, the fellow now known as Gutierrez thought. *Traitors are swine*. He would take pleasure in snuffing the life out of this one.

***

Washington is an international city and a man with a foreign driver's license and a valid passport can find a rental car with minimum fuss. He stopped at a strip mall near Annapolis and went into a hardware store and a supermarket to purchase the items he needed. He stopped at Sandy Point State Park on the Chesapeake Bay to assemble his parts and ingredients.

By sunset, he was crossing the Choptank River on Route 50. He used a hand-held GPS device to find a small frame house near the water and parked on the street. The front yard was enclosed by a rusting chain link fence. The steps up to the sagging porch were rotting and were held up by cinder blocks. The place had a derelict feel.

There were no curbs or sidewalks and vehicles—older pickups mostly—were parked at odd angles and the setting sun had cooled the air, sending the few people who were outside into their homes.

Gutierrez, as he would be known to everyone he met, was wearing a Washington Nationals baseball cap, jeans, and a hoody. He stood out only because most of the other men on the block wore Orioles caps. Hispanics were common on the Eastern Shore, working in chicken processing plants and the few seafood operations still in business. He would not be remembered.

***

Dave Haggard was travelling on Route 50, heading east to Ocean City. He was sick of the place. He was not a beach person and his tolerance for the sand and surf was limited to three days. After that, he was bored and confined himself indoors to read and drink. He had been holed up in a condo for the entire summer, recovering from his gunshot wound, and he was like a caged animal. Elena, on the other hand, loved the beach and spent her days marinating in the sun as her copper skin became a rich brown. She wanted to remain at the beach as long as possible. He had long ago vowed that he would never spend another day oiled and sand-covered.

He was on his way to tell her he was going back to Washington and back to work at Now News. He was its ace street reporter, the guy who got his hands dirty digging out the stories that well-dressed and well-shod media 'show-ponies' in the Capital wouldn't touch. It had made him famous. It had nearly killed him. Elena would not be happy.

His thoughts were back on the street as he crossed the Choptank at Cambridge, near where the river empties into the bay. It was getting dark and the air was cooling as he raised his driver's window. The radio was off. He felt peaceful and happy.

The explosion near the water rocked the car and sent it into the oncoming lane, narrowly missing a pickup going west. The vehicles on the bridge swerved to avoid each other and several careened into the jersey barriers that kept them from plunging into the water. To the right, toward the bay, a column of black smoke rose and drifted over the town. The cars on the bridge stopped where they were and the drivers got out to ask each other what had happened and to watch the smoke rise.

Dave's street reporter instincts kicked in and he drove around the other vehicles, crossed the bridge, and made a right turn into the neighborhood where the smoke was beginning to thin. People were in the streets, moving to the block where a fire engine was attempting to navigate the confusion. Dave and the fire fighters arrived at the same time and he stood in the street and gazed at the ruins of the house. Two dwellings on either side were partially collapsed and on fire, and a cargo van in front of the house was burning.

More fire units were arriving and the sound of air horns and sirens drowned out the noise of neighbors who were screaming and crying. A police car tried to part the crowd in the street and the cop at the wheel used the car's public address system to order everyone away from the scene. Dave pulled his D.C. press pass out of his wallet and waved it in front of the officer, who looked at it and ordered him to the other side of the street.

He pressed the record command on his smart phone and walked around the crowd, asking if anyone had seen the explosion. It was not a neighborhood where residents sought publicity, given that many of them were on shaky immigration status and others would rather not let the world know where they were staying. One man stepped forward.

"I saw it," the man said. "It went up just like that. Boom. No warning."

"Did you see anyone inside?"

"I don't know. I was just passing through. I don't live here."

"May I have your name?"

"Gutierrez. That's all I want to say." The man had a Spanish accent that contained an odd tonal quality.

Dave watched him walk away into the crowd. *Well,* he thought, *I have a quick sound bite.* "Boom. Just like that." It was something. Like most others in the crowd, Dave assumed the explosion was a gas leak or something similar. He waited and watched as other reporters arrived and set up their live shots. A television crew from Salisbury arrived first, led by a standard-issue TV blond woman and a middle-aged, pot-bellied cameraman. A young reporter from an Eastern Shore weekly newspaper walked up to the smoking pile of house parts, snapping photos with his phone.

A fire department Captain ordered the news media to stay together and away from the scene while his men and women hosed down the house. He huddled with a few of the firefighters and turned to the reporters, who were like baby birds waiting for a worm. They turned on their lights and set their devices on "record" as he walked up to them and began to speak.

"We have one deceased, badly burned and partially dismembered. No ID. The remains will be taken to the state medical examiner in Baltimore."

"Any word on a cause," Dave asked.

"Right now it appears to be an explosion of unknown origin."

"Any theories? Gas?"

"There are no natural gas lines in this neighborhood."

"Do you think it was intentional?" the blond asked.

"That remains to be determined but it's something we're looking at."

"So this could be a murder," Dave said.

"Yes." The captain wore the expression of someone who was about to fall through the ice. "We don't really know anything right now."

For Dave it was nothing more than a local story but he felt good working it. It was like a warm-up game in the minor leagues before an injured player returned to the major league lineup. There was a public station in Salisbury that might want the story and he planned to stop there before heading on to Ocean City. It would be nice to be behind a microphone again, even if only to report on a local fire.

Chapter Five

Gutierrez, as he now thought of himself, was elated and in a mood to celebrate. He checked into a motel on the eastern end of the Bay Bridge and washed in an act of purification before his prayers. He consumed a bottle of spring water as his good feeling spread over him, satisfied that the traitor had been sent to Satan to suffer for all eternity. *God is good.*

He sat at a small desk and opened his laptop, using a motel code to access the wifi. He opened software to mask his location and his identity and then, laughing, he turned out the lights in Bethesda, Maryland, an affluent community bordering Northwest Washington. He left them off for seven-hundred-eighty-six seconds, just over thirteen minutes. 786. It is considered a holy number by many Muslims. It was not holy to this man because his teacher had told him it was heresy to consider it so, but he was instructed to speak to the infidels with this number to catch the attention of their so-called Muslim scholars. He wondered if these dolts would even notice, such was his contempt for them. *Sit in the dark and try to solve the puzzle.*

***

The power company controllers who watched the grid from their underground center stared in disbelief as the alarms sounded and the lights flashed in reaction to the outages. Security programs flashed warnings that the system was "unable to access" the functions that would turn the lights back on. One of the world's largest defense contractors, based along the Beltway, experienced a one minute outage before its generators kicked in. Walter Reed National Military Medical Center was out for five minutes before its on-campus power supply generated electricity needed to operate one of the nation's premier medical facilities. The homes of the wealthy and powerful went dark and their air conditioning went silent. Most people assumed it was just another summer power outage and the phone lines at Pepco, the local power company, lit up with calls from customers who claimed to be "fed up" with an unreliable power system.

Gutierrez, for all of his training and preparation, had no way of knowing that the reliability of the Washington area's power grid had been an ongoing concern in the wake of both winter and summer outages that had lasted for days, prompting power companies to issue televised apologies. His message, such as it was, was lost in a larger argument.

He was in a terrorist mindset, one that relied on mass reaction to produce the desired result. He assumed that turning off the electricity to a population that relied on their gadgets for their lives would result in mass anger, if not hysteria. His demonstration from a motel on the Eastern Shore had only produced phone calls and "here we go again" complaints and, in the end, relief that the power had only been out for a few minutes. In short, nobody really got his message. He didn't know that as he went to sleep with a smile on his face, assuming that the infidels were on the verge of panic.

***

Sid Slackey, from his perch as the director of Now News, didn't think the power story was worthy of airtime outside the Washington area. He was thankful there was a generator in the basement. He had a television in his office and watched Channel Four's anchor team interview a local power company executive explain that they were doing everything possible to resolve the issue. Wendy Rieger, a veteran reporter and anchor, was wearing an expression that said if the executive had been a schoolboy she would have sent him to his room.

"So you really don't know what's causing these outages?" she asked.

"We are using all means at our disposal to determine what is causing these outages. As you know, they are of short duration and are therefore hard to pinpoint."

"Is it possible that these outages are caused by someone outside the system? Perhaps some kind of attack on the grid?"

The executive's face went pale. He had been trained to avoid any hint of cyber-attacks or terrorist activity against the grid and Homeland Security had advised him to shut down any questioning along those lines. It would panic the populace, he was told, and alert those who might be responsible. Besides, he was further informed, there was no evidence at the moment that such a thing was occurring.

"I have no knowledge of that," he stammered.

Rieger smelled blood. The man was obviously rattled. His eyes rolled and he looked left and right as though seeking assistance or escape.

"But you've considered it," she said. It was not a question.

"Well, of course we've considered it but, as I said, there's no evidence of that at this point."

"The power goes off and on. It's happened all over the area. What other explanation is there?"

"Look, I think we're done here." The man had the looked of a cornered animal.

"One more question," Rieger said. "Do you believe it's a software problem?"

"It could be. We're looking into that. It appears to be, as a matter of fact."

"How secure is your software?"

"We have confidence in it, if that's what you're asking. We have a new security program that monitors all aspects of the grid in this area and beyond."

"Have you considered that this problem is a cyber-attack?" She pressed the issue again.

"It might be, yes." The man seemed to shrink in his suit.

"Don't you think that is something you should be sharing with the public?"

"I've been advised against that by Homeland Security. As I said, we really don't know what is happening."

Rieger had scored a victory but she was not smiling. It occurred to her and the other reporters who were watching that something very big might be happening and local power outages were only the beginning.

Sid sat up. "Holy shit!" he said. It was a statement being repeated in newsrooms and Homeland Security offices all over the city.

Chapter Six

F.B.I. Special Agent Milford "Bud" Ossening was sitting at his desk in the D.C. field office reading a report about an informant who claimed that a gang of Hondurans was running a credit card scam in Northern Virginia and the District. The scheme, according to the informant, duped illegal Hispanic immigrants into believing that they could obtain legal drivers' licenses by stealing and handing over credit cards lifted from the homes where the Hispanics were working as house cleaners or yard workers. Ossening laughed at the scheme and wondered how anyone could fall for it, but then he recalled that illegals typically fall for just about anything that claims to burrow them deeper into American life. The Washington area was populated by people who lived below the radar and who were easy prey.

He closed the file, grabbed a PostIt note, wrote, "further action" on it, and placed it in the Out box. It was late afternoon and he was thinking that an early run to the beach might be a good idea when his phone rang. It was D.C. Police Inspector O'Neil.

"To what to I owe the attention of the Metropolitan Police?" Ossening used the formal name of the D.C. Police.

"Have you been watching Channel Four?"

"Some of us have actual jobs and we don't sit around watching television."

"Well, some of us are paid to do nothing and we surf the Web or watch the lovely Wendy Rieger read the news. Speaking of Ms. Rieger, she just interviewed the Pepco guy and got him to say all of these spot outages we've had might be the work of bad guys. What do you know about that?"

"What do you mean bad guys?"

"As in terrorists, I assume."

"Pepco thinks terrorists are the cause of the black-outs? That's an interesting take on it. How come everyone else thinks it's tree limbs and storms?"

"Because we don't play well with others and share would be my guess. We seem to be back where we were before 9/11. Everybody's playing keepsees with information. I made a few calls and it seems Homeland is seriously looking into the terrorism angle." O'Neil's voice had moved from friendly to serious.

"Maybe a call to us would be nice," Ossening said. "I'll pass this up the pipe."

"Have you ever wondered why you weren't invited to party that all your friends went to?"

Ossening offered O'Neil a smirk. "Not really. They wonder why they aren't invited to parties I go to."

"Are you on somebody's shit list?"

"And your meaning?"

"Things change."

"I'll let you know if I get transferred to the field office in Boise."

***

Patricia Gant was in her own version of Boise. She was occupying a drab office in an abandoned building on the grounds of the old Walter Reed Army Medical Center on land situated between 16th Street and Georgia Avenue in upper Northwest Washington. The new Walter Reed, now dubbed the Walter Reed National Military Medical Center, was located on the grounds of what had been known as the Bethesda National Naval Medical Center in Maryland. A base realignment commission had determined that the federal government could save money by combining its two premier military medical facilities into one. The idea that such a combination would save even one dollar had long been abandoned, and millions were spent to create the new facility whose prime impact had been to create monumental traffic jams in Bethesda as staff, patients and visitors inserted themselves onto already-crowded Wisconsin Avenue, creating ill-will and demands that the federal government spend even more money to building new roads.

Gant was not concerned about such things as she stared at the peeling government-green paint on the wall next to her government-issue metal desk. She was having a moment of reflection about her career, such as it was. She was the daughter of an Air Force colonel, an expert on cyber security, who had died in the Pentagon on 9/11. Colonel Gant was the finest man she had ever known. He had endured the racism that permeated the services when he was a young officer, he had distinguished himself at the Air Force Academy, and he obtained a PhD from

M.I.T. He was honest, committed, and devoted to his daughter and had tears in his eyes when she graduated with top honors at Harvard's Law School. The world was hers for the taking.

9/11 changed everything. She walked out of a Manhattan white stocking law firm and into the F.B.I. school at Quantico, vowing to devote her life to fighting the evil that had taken her father and so many others on that horrible day. What she had not considered was her own aggressive nature. Power and influence at the F.B.I. flows down, not up, and swimmers against the tide are given the jobs that no one wants. Some agents refer to it as "being assigned to count the cars in the garage."

So here she was, watching the paint peel in a dead-end job in a backwater Homeland Security office on an abandoned piece of ground. At least parking was not a problem.

The phone on her desk rang with its outdated ringtone. Even the phones are throwaways, she thought, as she picked it up. "Gant."

"O'Neil here. I've just had a chat with a colleague of yours. He seems to think he's out of the loop on this and that. Got time for a cup of coffee?"

"I've got time to grow the beans. Any word on Rodell Clark?"

"Not yet. I think some of yours are working with Virginia cops on it. My guess is he's flown the coop. He could be in Costa Rica by now. Dulles is only a few minutes from where he took off."

"Anybody see him at Dulles?"

"Not that I've heard but that doesn't mean much."

"Meet me at the deli at 22nd and P. Give me fifteen minutes."

She had been assigned a three-year-old Ford sedan that been designed for low level federal employees, who, despite their lowly status, were deemed to need transportation. The vehicle did not even have a radio. It was as basic and plain as it got in Detroit these days. It bore federal government tags and black, plain wheels. Gant would rather have taken the bus, but, in theory, she was always available to respond to calls from the Bureau, so she drove down 16th Street to P, cut over to 22nd, and spent a few minutes looking for a meter. D.C. had installed meters that took credit cards, so she used her F.B.I. plastic to run up a three dollar tab to be picked up by America's taxpayers.

O'Neil was outside, sneaking a smoke and staring at a young woman sporting a blue Mohawk and tattoos that covered all of her exposed upper body, which was most of it. Only her nipples were covered with spangled stars.

"Getting an eye full?" Gant looked at O'Neil with a raised eyebrow.

"How'd you like your daughter to turn up like that?" He threw the cigarette into the street.

"Is she your daughter?"

"No chance."

"Then let it go. It's hot out here, let's go inside."

The place was half filled with twenty-somethings wearing thick, black hipster glasses and standard-issue khaki shorts. They all were staring at screens, either phones, tablets or laptops.

"Parallel play," Gant whispered. "Notice how quiet it is. They get along with others."

They took seats in a corner and O'Neil got to the point. "Homeland thinks there's a terrorist connection to the blackouts. Your man Ossening is not in on the loop. What do you think?"

"We're not, either, and we're the ones who lost the doer." Gant was wearing her lawyer face.

O'Neil stared at her and allowed himself to see her as a strikingly beautiful woman. His brain hit the pause button and he was quiet.

Gant leaned forward. "Hello? Anyone home?"

"Sorry. I was thinking about something else."

"Don't tell me."

"I think we can work this thing but we have to stick together. That means not carrying too much water for those who think we're here on ice. Get my drift?"

"Is that supposed to be some kind of metaphor?"

"Like I said, get my drift?"

"You and me against the world? Yeah sure. Why not? What are they gonna do, send me to Walter Reed?"

Chapter Seven

The man who called himself Gutierrez avoided cell phones, email and all over-the-air communication. "They are watching and listening," he was told. It was decided that his handlers would communicate the old fashioned way, with coded, written messages hidden in out-of-the-way locations. His superiors had seen Cold War spy movies and thought that scraps of paper under rocks and coded marks on trees were better methods of passing instructions and warnings. "The Internet is a nest of American spies," they said. "Why do you think they invented it? Look what it has done to our people."

And so he found himself in Ocean City, Maryland, sitting on a bench overlooking the beach, gagging on the scent of greasy French fries. Families strolled by with their children, young women shamelessly showed off their bodies, young men playfully shoved each other and pointed to the young women, and the man on the bench waited. He prayed to Allah that the filthy rabble walking by would be struck down and exiled to the fires of Hell for all eternity.

The sun was high when another man sat down on the bench and placed a large cup of fried potatoes between him and Gutierrez. Nothing was said between them. Neither man looked at the other. After a period of about ten minutes the stranger walked away, leaving the cup. Five minutes after that Gutierrez stood, picked up the cup, and strolled to the rooming house where he had paid for a small room.

The message in the cup was short and simple. Return to Washington and go to Rock Creek Park in two days.

***

Twenty blocks away, along Ocean City's Gold Coast, Dave Haggard was standing on a balcony a dozen stories above the beach, stroking the hair of a golden-skinned woman who was angry. Her name was Elena Romona-Cayo. She was small and carried herself with a dignity that made men ashamed of the thoughts they had for her. She could have any man she desired and it confused and disturbed her that she wanted Dave, whom she viewed as reckless and irresponsible. She also found him to be irresistible. Her attraction to him had nearly cost her life. The fading scar on her face was proof of that. A fiendish killer had come close to "sacrificing" her in fevered religious lunacy that Dave had brought her into as part of a story he was working on.

"You're not ready to go back," she said. She did not look at him.

"I can't stand this anymore. It's boring. Some people like the beach. I like the smell of bus fumes in the city." He tried to lighten the mood but she pulled away.

"Did you like the feeling of the bullet that almost killed you in Tennessee?"

"Let's not go over that again. We've been here for weeks. I'm fine."

"Maybe I'm not fine, Dave. Maybe I need more time to heal myself. Do you ever think about me?"

"I think about you every day. I'm not a house cat, Elena. I can't lounge around all day every day and watch the tide come in."

"Why don't you write a book or something. That will occupy your mind."

"I'm a street reporter."

"You're a prick."

"That, too."

"And an asshole."

"Okay, a prick and an asshole."

"What do you want from me?" She turned to face him. "What's next for us? Do not say we'll get back to normal. There is no normal here."

"What do you want?" Dave's brain hit the pause button whenever Elena took them into emotional territory.

She stared at him with a look of disgust. "I'll call Sid and tell him we're coming back to work."

"Thank you," he said, trying to hug her.

She moved away and walked into the bedroom, slamming the door. He sat in one of the plastic chairs on the balcony and watched the people on the beach roast themselves in the sun, and wondered how they could stand to be hot and idle for hours on end.

Two hours later his phone rang. It was O'Neil. The two men had an up and down history, not uncommon among reporters and their sources. Each had betrayed the other and each had helped the other. O'Neil had once described it as two scorpions in a jar. Dave thought the description was too harsh.

"So, Scribe, how goes the battle?" O'Neil was trying to sound upbeat and was failing.

"Scribes are the newspaper guys. What's up?"

"When are you going to start earning your keep?"

"Funny you should ask."

"We should talk."

"About anything in particular?"

"Not on the phone."

***

Dave's apartment was near Dupont Circle on a block of Massachusetts Avenue that housed a famous think tank, a university foreign policy program, a few embassies and several condo buildings that had been converted in the early eighties. It was a block where English was just another language in the air. The lobby was classy in a casual, international style and the desk was staffed by Cameroonians who attended Howard University. No one could remember exactly when the Cameroonians took over, but they were polite, spoke several languages, and took care of the residents, so there was never a suggestion that they be replaced. They had all committed the names of the residents and their regular guests to memory.

"Mr. Haggard! Welcome home! How are you feeling?" The man behind the desk was thin, coal black, and elegant as he approached Dave with an outstretched hand and a concerned face.

"I'm fine, James. I've had enough beaches to last a lifetime. Anything for me?"

"We have your mail in a box and there's a note for you that was left by your police friend." The Cameroonians all knew O'Neil on sight.

Dave took his mail to his apartment and left the box on the table. He opened the note from O'Neil. "Coffee. Six." He looked at his watch and saw that he had over an hour. He went through his mail and separated out the overdue bills from the credit card offers, charity solicitations, and fliers from Gay Pride groups.

An hour later Dave walked into the Keener Beaner and saw O'Neil sitting in a corner, raising his hand. The place was a Hipster coffee hangout and nearly everyone was wearing glasses with thick black frames. Most of them were in their twenties and they stared at their phones or tablets, ignoring everyone else. Dave maneuvered his way past a young woman who was having an argument with a young man whose face was shouting at her from a smartphone screen.

"Welcome to the future," O'Neil said, offering his hand. "You could machinegun half of these people and the others wouldn't notice."

"How's the face?" Dave looked at O'Neil for signs of a nearly fatal beating the Inspector, then a captain, had suffered at the hands of a particularly brutal hit man who favored brass knuckles in his work.

"Handsome as ever. How's the bullet wound?"

"Coming along. I'm going back to work. Living at the beach is a kind of death."

O'Neil held up his cell phone and made a show of putting it in his pants pocket. He leaned over and whispered, "I have something for you, a nice story that can get your blood moving again."

"Not another lunatic hit man. I've been there and done that."

"Put your phone in your pocket." O'Neil pointed to Dave's phone on the table and waited while he stashed it in the front pocket of his jeans. "Okay, how about a terrorist who wants to turn out the lights and maybe has a way to do it?"

"You have details?"

"That's where you come in."

Dave broke into a smile. "Son of a bitch! Let's go to my place and we can talk."

"Not so fast, Scribe. Let's leave our phones at the desk in your building and go for a private walk." O'Neil raised his eyebrows and pointed to his ear. "Let's find some private space."

Chapter Eight

The man who called himself Gutierrez paid another visit to the mosque on Massachusetts Avenue, offering his prayers and fealty, and walked into Rock Creek Park to a spot overlooking a bike path. Two gay men were on a blanket, kissing and staring at each other, and he felt an urge to kill them both for what he believed to be a violation of all that was holy. He closed his eyes and took deep breaths, telling himself that he was on a holy mission and that sinners would be brought to their rightful punishment. The gay men glanced at him and laughed, waving.

He found a cleared area where a stone had been marked with a small chevron. Beneath the stone was a plastic bag that contained a single wrinkled piece of paper. There were no words on the paper, only symbols instructing him to perform several tasks. He smiled and felt a moment of jubilation. Yes! He had been chosen. He sank to his knees in gratitude. Then he rose and walked out onto Massachusetts Avenue, where he caught a bus that took him to a Metro station, where he rode the train into Virginia. He made his way to a lot where he rented a van. He drove the van to Winchester, where he scouted several golf courses, noting storage buildings. He would need several tons of ingredients and it would take him time to gather it without calling attention to himself or his mission.

***

Dave felt alive for the first time in weeks. His wound was almost healed and he had a great story to work on. His first task was to find out what Homeland Security was thinking and whether someone there really believed a terrorist was playing with the Washington area's power grid. The federal government would never admit that it had been outsmarted and would try to keep something like that under wraps until it had a solution and an arrest or a dead terrorist. Who else knew?

Recent revelations that the government had been snooping on journalists had produced the usual howls from the usual news organizations but these so-called "revelations" were not news to most of Washington's street reporters. It had been a dark secret for years and was the topic of late-night bar conversation. The journalists who covered the national security beat had made no secret of their troubles with F.B.I. agents who followed them around, tapped phones, monitored Internet use and employed any other device the government could use to keep tabs on them. National security correspondents assumed that everything they did was in a data base at N.S.A. and they acted accordingly, using go-betweens to exchange confidential information. In a way, these reporters waved and said, "Hey, N.S.A.! Look at me!" while their less conspicuous colleagues did the work of ferreting out the details of activities the government would rather be left unlit.

The national security reporters allowed themselves to be shown what the government wanted them to see and to be flown on government planes to the places where the government wanted to put on a pony show, including Afghanistan, the Horn of Africa, and certain places in South America. These pony shows did not extend to surveillance activities in the Nation's Capital. Nor did they include anything that might embarrass Homeland Security, the current administration, or key members of Congress.

A select group of reporters in Washington were the keepers of secrets and knew where bones were buried. These journalists were experienced diggers and had been on their beats for years, covering the mundane, day-to-day business of government in all its forms. One of these reporters was Dave McConnell, who for decades had covered Congress for WTOP, the city's all-news station. In a city obsessed with news, WTOP was not only the top rated station but was also the highest grossing radio station in America. In a town where news is made, news is also money.

Dave McConnell knew more about the workings of Congress than most of its members, including a good portion of the leadership. It was not unusual for a key member to ask Dave a procedural question or advice on matters of legislation. McConnell knew all of the key members of the Intelligence committees and knew the rumors in the air and which ones seemed to have something to ground them. Dave found him in the correspondent's gallery, a warren of cubicles and electronic gear. McConnell was editing some audio and writing several reports about pending legislation to be aired on the station later that day.

McConnell was unfailingly polite, a rare trait in the news business, and he greeted Dave with a serious smile.

"Long time no see. How are you?"

"I'm going nuts on the beach," Dave said. "I'm back in the salt mine and I need to talk to you about something."

"Give me ten minutes," McConnell said. "I need to get these filed." The pieces were run-of-the-mill news gruel about various issues in Congress and did not mention any actual legislation, given that members of the House and Senate had retreated into a kind of kindergarten behavior involving finger pointing, food fights, "He started it!" The business of governing had been left aside.

Dave caught up on local newsroom gossip and any Congressional issues that might touch upon the Justice Department, which was his beat, at least in the past, before he was shot.

McConnell sat back, glancing at his screen for messages or notices of news conferences, statements, or, as unlikely as it was, Congressional action on anything. "I'm assuming you're not here to chat. What's on your mind?"

"Are you hearing anything about terrorists being behind these weird power outages? Any rumors or whispers from Intelligence Committee types?"

"No, not up here. In fact, some members are suggesting that the power guy's comments to Wendy Rieger were just empty attempts to look as though they're on top of things. No one seems to be taking it seriously."

"I have sources who are taking it seriously, although they don't appear to have anything hard on it."

"I don't suppose you'd be willing to share those sources." McConnell was smiling.

"No, but I'll make a deal with you. I'll pass along what I hear, unattributed, if you'll do the same."

"Okay, you're on." McConnell glanced at his screen and stood up, "Gotta run. The Speaker's going to say something. Who knows? It might actually be newsworthy." He grabbed his coat and audio kit bag and ran for the door.

Dave looked around at the cramped gallery and smiled. It was great to be back in the craziness, feeling the energy and the sarcasm.

One of the network correspondents had posted what appeared to be an official memo from headquarters in New York. "Due to travel budget cuts, all round trips to Miami will terminate in Atlanta." The signature was Adolph Hitler.

Chapter Nine

The Honorable Peter Z. Taylor was the lowest ranking member of either party on The Permanent Select
Committee on Intelligence in the United States House of
Representatives. Intel, as those who saw themselves as
insiders referred to it, was a hot assignment in the age of
terrorism. Taylor was thirty-one years old, a war hero, a
top graduate of the Yale law school, and the latest in a
line of Southerners who traced their genes to the twelfth
President of the United States, Zachary Taylor, whose
offspring had provided the Congressmen with the Z as his
middle initial.

Taylor was the winner of a special election in East
Tennessee following the murder of John Prewitt, Jr., a
morally-challenged member of a prominent family. The
late Congressman Prewitt had been the victim of one of
his co-conspirators in a scheme to defraud the United
States Treasury out of millions of dollars in environmen-
tal cleanup money.

Taylor had never expressed a strong political opinion
about anything, a quality he shared with his ancestor
Zachary, who, despite having no discernible political be-
liefs, was elected President on the good will generated by
his heroic record in the war with Mexico.

Peter had been an Army Ranger in Iraq and won a Silver Star and Purple Heart on his first deployment. He was assigned to Army Intelligence on his second deployment and was wounded again, ending his military career. His war record and his high standing at Yale Law made him a hot property at Knoxville's top firms and he enjoyed a brief and happy phase as a hotshot lawyer with a golden pedigree until the local grandees decided he would make an ideal candidate for Congress. He went along with it, assuming he could satisfy the right people by running, lose, and return to his happy life. He won.

His backers had touted his experience in Iraq as justification for his assignment on Intel. They and the party leadership assumed he thought like they did, to the far right, and would be a convenient vote on their side, never making waves or asking uncomfortable questions. After all, they reasoned, he never expressed an opinion about politics, so he must be one of us.

Peter Taylor was smart and quiet. His time as an Army Ranger had made him tough, his assignment to Army Intelligence had made him wary, and law school had organized his mind. He was no one's patsy.

Dave Haggard found him in his office, eating a sandwich at his desk. A staffer waved him in.

"Hello, Congressman. Got a minute?"

Taylor had only a vague idea who Dave was and recalled that he had been shot in what was now his district but he seemed like a nice guy so he pointed to a chair. "Have a seat."

"Welcome to Washington," Dave said. "I won't take much of your time. Are you hearing any rumors about what's behind the power outages in the area? Anything raise any alarms?"

Taylor raised his eyebrows. "Tell me more."

"I don't know if there is more. The power company guy says it might be terrorism. Have you heard that?"

"Well, Mr. Haggard, what I hear or don't hear is not for public consumption."

"Is that a yes or a no?"

"Just between us, I haven't heard anything like that. Where did you get it?"

"It's been on the news but it's been denied everywhere. It's one of those Washington rumors that get spread around."

"Maybe that's all it is, a rumor."

Dave stood up and headed for the door. "Thank you for your time."

It was just another in a dozen such encounters every day, informal polling about issues, rumors, gossip and the odd chance that something was happening that was newsworthy.

Taylor finished his sandwich and picked up the phone. An hour later he was sitting in a booth in a diner at Tysons Corner in Virginia, across from a large man who wore an Army field hat that bore the wings of a paratrooper and the tab of a Ranger. The man was no longer a soldier. He was a contractor who worked out of a secret facility in what was informally called the Dulles Corridor, a region of high tech, super-secret operations and public companies enjoying the free flow of taxpayer dollars alleged to be in the interests of the nation. The man listened as Taylor relayed the rumor.

"What did they tell us at Intel school? There's no such thing as a coincidence? Let me see what I can come up with. I'll run these outages through a pattern program. Meet me here tomorrow."

The two men stood and shook hands. "Rangers lead the way," Taylor said. It was the Ranger motto.

***

Twenty-four hours later the men sat at the same booth and Taylor read a one-page assessment. The Washington area's power grid was under the control of an unknown person or persons. Homeland Security was aware and working on a fix. The White House had not been informed. Nor had Congress. The hope was that the problem could be made to go away before any real damage was done.

"Odds?" Taylor asked.

"They're playing defense at Homeland. The play is on the other side. My guess is the power thing is only part of the game. The problem here is the lack of commo intel. Sigint hasn't picked up anything on this. These guys are doing it the old fashioned way. We need boots on the ground to find them." The lack of communications intelligence and signal intelligence meant that there was no traffic for the NSA or anyone else to intercept. No cell phone chatter, no Internet communications, nothing.

"This is where it gets interesting," Taylor said.

"You gonna tell your friends on the Hill?"

"They don't give a shit about this. They'll just use it to bash the other side, then they'll go out for a drink. Let's keep this close."

"Roger that."

Taylor drove to a nondescript office park near Dulles and made his way to a small basement office. He logged in to a secure server, spent an hour accessing files, and was back in his office by five-thirty for an appointment with the Intelligence Committee chairman, who wanted to spend a few minutes going over the rules. Taylor listened politely, committed to nothing, and went to dinner at a sushi place, where he went unnoticed.

Chapter Ten

Patricia Gant hated reporters. It was a hatred born of her father's opinion that journalists were all working their own agendas and her own experience with legal reporters who, in her opinion, never understood the law. She was not happy to be sitting across the table from Dave Haggard at the invitation of Inspector O'Neil, who seemed to have some kind of relationship with him. *Never a good idea,* she thought.

To Gant, Dave had a bit of a Southern cracker in him. It wasn't just the accent. He had the look of someone raised in the Old South, a slouch, a gaze, something that said he poured peanuts into his Coke.

"So, Mr. Haggard, how do you see this? Is there a story here?" She looked at him with the expression of someone who was amused and bored at the same time.

"Not yet," Dave said. "It doesn't look like anyone's following up on it. The Redskins are starting the season and the Nationals are in a pennant race, so rumors about the power being out aren't big news. It's only news if it's out and even that only to the people who are sitting in the dark."

"So you don't see anything there."

"Like I said, not yet."

O'Neil was watching this and growing impatient. "What if I told you Homeland thinks there something there."

"Did they tell you that?"

"Sort of."

"I sort of asked around on the Hill and nothing."

"Okay, how about this?" O'Neil said, sitting back and crossing his arms over his chest. "I have news for you. Do you remember an explosion over on the Eastern Short, in Cambridge? I think you were there. A guy died."

"Gas leak, as I recall."

"Well, the guy was named Rodell Clark. I'll bet you never heard of him."

"No, should I?"

"Not really. Agent Gant and I had a very brief chat with Mr. Clark a few hours before he died. We think he knew something about the power outages. He fled our questioning and turned up as burnt toast in a cheap neighborhood near the Bay. As an experienced street reporter, how do you read it?" O'Neil was wearing his smirk.

"Why were you questioning him?" Dave took out his phone to turn on the record function.

"Ah, no. We're not going to do that again." O'Neil held up his hands. "Put the phone in your pocket. You've burned me with that crap before. No recording anything."

Gant looked at O'Neil and shook her head. "We shouldn't be here."

"You were telling me why you were questioning Clark." Dave made a show of sliding the phone into his front pants pocket.

"No, I wasn't," O'Neil said. "I will tell you this. He's the guy who was supposed to write the code to protect the system and he was there when all of this started. Just a friendly tip. If I were an enterprising reporter looking for a scoop, I would do some looking around at the life and times of Rodell Clark."

"What do you want from me?"

"Just keep in touch, like always."

Chapter Eleven

Argun Maskhadov was as happy as he had ever been. His plan was working and he was allowing himself a moment of satisfaction and fantasy. He sat back and inhaled the smoke from the hookah, feeling the warmth and grit of the tobacco. He laughed. *Here am I, thousands of miles from my miserable home, in the company of these infidels who live in ways unimaginable to my people. Suffering is its own reward, we were told. Well, my friends, you will soon have your reward.*

Argun Maskhadov was Chechen by birth, radical Muslim by faith, and bitter by experience. He had spent his childhood in a refugee camp in Ingushetia, a miserable Russian republic next door to even more miserable Chechnya. His family had been driven out by marauding Russian troops sent to end—by any means—the rebellion against Moscow's rule. Citizens of Ingushetia were happy to have Argun and his fellow Chechens to look down upon and called them dogs and sons of whores and worse.

Maskhadov had fled as a boy of fifteen and found his way to Pakistan where he was tested in ways that left him scarred and strong. He was clever and he was pleased to learn that he had no conscience when it came to the suffering of others. In fact, he found a measure of satisfaction in manipulating others to achieve his own aims, even it produced pain and suffering in those around him.

He once read an American self-help book that instructed him to visualize his dreams and goals and to see himself achieving all that he dreamt of. Dream big, he was told, and reach for the stars. *Yes!* He thought and laughed again.

***

The hookah bar was in Frederick, Maryland, a small city fifty miles from Washington. It was a distant suburb that attracted young people who worked for the companies that were fed, one way or another, from the trough of federal cash that spilled up Interstate 270. The older part of the city dated to the late 18th Century and had been reclaimed as a charming downtown with trendy restaurants and the hookah bar, where young Americans pretended to be sophisticated as they smoked and drank expensive juice drinks.

Maskhadov smiled at them and tried to be charming and friendly. Right now they were not his concern. He needed a place to be and this was it for the moment. He turned his thoughts to Ikram Ali Ghazali, also known as Gutierrez. The man was very stupid, that much was evident. But he was being useful and following instructions, more or less, and that counted in his favor. Maskhadov knew he would have to convince the man to avoid the mosque. That would be difficult for a devout believer but he had to convince him that it was in the service of the cause. Maskhadov knew that if anyone was watching the Ghazali they would find it strange that a man named

Gutierrez worshipped at the Islamic Center and not at a Catholic church.

Maskhadov smiled at the knowledge that Ikram Ali Ghazali was a diversion, a way to make the Americans believe one thing was happening while another was about to destroy them. Ghazali was unaware of his role and so was taking his tasks to heart. *Let him turn off the lights,* Maskhadov mused, *and let the Americans chase him down. All will be known in time.* He recalled the Arab proverb: *'A mule that goes in search of a fine set of antlers will come back with his ears cut off'.*

Maskhadov left the hookah bar and walked to his room, where he wrote new instructions for the man called Gutierrez. He drove a rental car into Washington and parked off Military Road. He walked down into the park and waved to a woman on the bridle path, complementing her on the fine horse she was astride. The woman noticed his bright smile and waved back. *What a fool*, he thought. *In Chechnya I could buy this woman for less than her horse.*

He placed the message under a plastic rock and walked back to his car. He drove to Southeast Washington where he took pictures of one of America's premier baseball stadiums. He wore a bright red Nationals cap and appeared to be just another fan eager to watch a game. The first pitch was hours away but there were police and security people in evidence at the gates and on the streets. *I have work to do*, he thought.

***

The man who called himself Gutierrez retrieved the message and took it to his room. He was puzzled by it and spent an hour in prayer hoping the Divine would make it clear to him. He was being told to avoid anything that could identify him as a Believer, even the Mosque. How could he, a man on a Holy Mission, fail to show his devotion? He lay back on his bed and drifted into a deep sleep. He dreamt that he was an angel flying through brilliant white clouds to a garden where virgins were waiting to pleasure him and feed him sweet fruit. He felt light and happy and knew that he was in Paradise. He did not want to leave.

The dream was interrupted by a loud knocking on his door and he felt helpless as the dream drifted away and he returned to his miserable live on Earth. He wanted to die at that moment and return to Paradise and the virgins and the sweet fruit. He was angry at the person who dared to bring him back.

He stormed to the door and pulled it open. There, with a frightened look, stood the bus driver from the tour company, holding his suitcase.

"*Dejaste tu bolso, señor.*" You left your bag, Sir. The driver held the suitcase out so the man who called himself Gutierrez could take possession of it.

"*Idiota. Yo estaba durmiendo.*" Idiot! I was sleeping.

"*Lo siento. Perdóname, por favor.*" I am sorry. Please forgive me. The driver set the suitcase in the doorway and fled.

The man who called himself Gutierrez grabbed the bag and threw it onto the bed. He closed his eyes and tried to bring back the feeling of Paradise, but it was gone, lost to the knock on the door and his encounter with the driver. He saw the dream as a Divine message instructing him to carry out his mission and enter Paradise forever. He would not go to the Mosque and he would disguise his faith as instructed in the absolute trust that his reward would be fulfilled.

He set down his prayer rug, washed himself, and wept as he prayed in thankful devotion. He then opened his laptop and turned out the lights in Northwest Washington and Old Town Alexandria.

***

Deep in an underground complex beneath Tysons Corner in the Virginia suburbs, a small team of cyber experts tracked the outages back to Gutierrez's laptop. They replicated his keystrokes and watched his curser move across the screen. Within seconds they had copied the program that allowed him to take control of the electric grid and within an hour they knew who had been responsible for its creation. The man who called himself Gutierrez was in the trap. He was the goat tied to the stake. The team alerted others who would watch and wait for the lion to come to the goat.

Chapter Twelve

Dave Haggard called Inspector O'Neil, hoping for a story he could put on the air. O'Neil answered the call hoping Dave had some bit of information that would help him move the case of the power outages forward into an investigation that would at least be interesting. Both men were disappointed.

"I talked to a guy on the Intelligence Committee and he hadn't heard anything," Dave said.

"You can't possibly think that anyone who knows anything would tell some reporter who just happens to walk through the door," O'Neil said, sounding bored.

"I believed him. I also talked to Dave McConnell and he says there aren't any rumors about terrorists behind the power outages."

"How would he know?"

"He's been covering Congress since Millard Filmore."

"So what."

"McConnell knows more about Congress than half the members up there."

"Everyone knows more than half the members. Those guys can't put on their own pants. As for me, I don't have anything new. Neither does Gant. We're back to pushing paper at each other. Keep in touch." O'Neil ended the call and turned to Gant. "He doesn't know," he said.

"Let's keep it that way," Gant replied.

***

Dave took a cab to Capitol Hill and went to the offices of the Honorable Peter Z. Taylor of Tennessee. He was fishing for anything he could catch, whether it related to the power outages or not. He didn't care if he got a story out of the visit. He liked the feeling of being back on the street and talking to someone who was part of the Washington game, even one as lowly at Taylor.

The Congressman was in his office, reading a pile of bills that his party leaders wanted passed, or at least considered in committee. Most of them were not worthy of much attention but the leaders felt the rank and file should be on record as supporting them when the next campaign came around which, in the current political climate, was always right now. Taylor, for his part, was bored with all of it and longed to get back to his comfortable legal life and bachelor perks that came with it, not that entertainment of a female persuasion was not available in Washington. It was there, but there were too many cautions and too many reporters snooping around to make the game worthwhile.

Dave's arrival gave him a break from the tedium and he waved him in. "So, fellow Tennessean, how goes the battle?" He pointed to a chair.

Dave sat and looked at Taylor. He saw a good looking Southerner who had the air of a man who was smarter than he wanted to appear. He smiled from the nose down but his eyes were alert.

"I'm just getting back into it," Dave said. "How's it with you?"

"Can't complain about doing the people's business, Dave."

"Hear anything interesting?" Dave threw his line in the water.

"About?"

"The power problem. Any more on the terrorist angle?"

Taylor looked at Dave for a full minute without speaking. "I've been asking around about you. You have a mixed record in the trust department."

"How's that?"

"I hear you've broken a few confidences. This police friend of yours, O'Neil, I hear you burned him on an off the record conversation."

Dave was surprised that Taylor had bothered to ask around about him and even more startled to hear that his use of an accidental recording of a conversation with O'Neil had come up. "It was not intentional," Dave said.

"These things never are," Taylor replied before Dave could explain. "But you have a pretty good reputation with others, so maybe we can come to an understanding. You with me?"

"I don't know. What kind of understanding do you have in mind?"

"From now on everything is off the record. If you burn me I will deny to my dying breath anything you reveal and I will do all I can to nail your ass to a barn door.

Understood?" Taylor said it with a smile on his face but his tone was serious.

"Got it," Dave said. "What's on your mind?"

"First, it appears that someone is manipulating the electric grid and hoping we'll panic or make a big deal out of it. It also appears that they have failed in that regard, given that most people see it as another pain in the ass and not something to send us screaming into the streets. Frankly, I don't know or even care whether other members of the Intelligence Committee are aware of it. I doubt it and I have no intention of telling them. Some of them couldn't keep a secret if their lives depended on it. My sources are outside the committee and let's leave it at that."

"Why are you telling me?"

"Background. Keep it to yourself. The shit storm that was kicked up when Wendy Rieger talked to the Pepco guy seems to have died out for lack of supporting evidence, so we'll let it lie for now."

"Why would you care what I have for background?"

"Because I suspect there's more on the way and I want one guy around here who knows what's going on. Let's keep it at that right now. I want to see if what I told you turns up in the news in the next couple of days. If it does, I'll know where it came from and you're screwed. If it doesn't we can have another conversation. Deal?" Taylor stood up.

"One question. What do you mean when you say more on the way?"

"Like I said, we'll talk another day."

Dave left Taylor's office wondering whether he had a story or just the beginning of one. He hailed a cab back to Now News. He needed to talk to Sid.

Chapter Thirteen

Agent Milford "Bud" Ossening had never been in any of the inner circles at the Bureau. Every posting, every department, every supervisor of any sort had, like most groups of human beings, a circle of people who were considered "one of us" or "on the team." Ossening had never been seen as a team guy, even though he was good at his work, showed up on time, looked the part, and did well at the schools to which the F.B.I. sent him. There was something about him, it was said, that was, well, weird.

Ossening was aware of all of this and tried not to concern himself with what he thought of as office politics. The practical effect was that he became the go-to guy for ordinary drudge work, tasks that others thought boring or not good for their careers.

And so Ossening steadily rose through the ranks of the F.B.I.'s worker bees, achieving a mid-level rank that paid well and kept him out of the line of fire in more ways that the obvious. He was given various liaison jobs with this task force or that multi-state committee. He came to know many people, some of whom at the face of the terrorist threats that went largely unknown to the general public. Ossening had connections that his superiors and those who dismissed him would covet, should they ever come to such knowledge.

Ossening was reading a report that made him smile. A cyber team that officially did not exist had tracked a man who had the ability to control the Washington area's electric grid and was responsible for the frequent but brief outages that had recently been in the news. The media had forgotten about the terrorist angle after nothing had been confirmed, sending the angle into the rumor bin. The team that had tracked the man was keeping an eye on him and working up the chain. There was nothing for Ossening to do but file the report alongside the others that came across his desk in case someone at the Bureau wanted to know if he had seen it.

His desk phone rang. It was O'Neil.

"Hello there, Special Agent. How's life at America's premier crime fighting organization?"

"Always good to hear from you, Inspector. What can the Bureau do for you today?"

"Just checking to see if anything has come up that I should know about." O'Neil was aware of Ossening's contacts.

"Let's see. Nope. Nothing here."

"How about Homeland's terrorist? Anything new there?"

"Which one. They have a lot of them."

"This one is the electricity guy."

"Maybe you should call them."

"Got time for coffee?" O'Neil smelled something.

Ossening knew that O'Neil had some hard information but the agent was not working the case, so he had no reason to become involved. On the other hand, he could use some fresh air. "Three o'clock. Meet me at the Navy Memorial."

The Navy Memorial was on Pennsylvania Avenue Northwest between 7th and 9th Streets. It's a plaza that contains two fountains, two ships masts, a map of the globe, and a statue of a lone sailor. It's a popular spot for office workers and tourists who want to sit and enjoy the city on nice days.

***

Ossening found O'Neil slurping a cold coffee drink on the steps between the fountains. "It's hot," O'Neil said by way of greeting.

"What's up?" Ossening sat next to O'Neil.

"Any idea who the guy is?" O'Neil asked. "Don't ask which guy."

"I'm not on the street," Ossening said. "Do some shoe leather work and use your sources."

"The thinking right now is this guy is too obvious. He might be a diversion. Everyone wants to know who he's working for. Any ideas?"

"I just push papers, Inspector. Everything you want to know is above my pay grade."

"Bullshit. You have access to all the dark closets. Agent Gant thinks very highly of you. Help us out here."

"Agent Gant is a shit-listee, like you. The Bureau hopes she will never be heard from again."

"She's a good agent and she smells something. So do I. Ask around, that's all I want."

"How are things with your friend Dave Haggard?"

"Why do you ask?"

"Give me a break. You met with him. You're playing him. How much does he know?"

"Nothing is my guess. How do you know we've been in contact?"

"Jesus, Inspector. Do you think anybody has any secrets anymore? You and Gant and Haggard and half this city are always being watched by somebody. I'll bet a ticket to a Nats game that interested parties already know we're sitting here."

***

Pennsylvania Avenue is monitored by a series of security cameras and other technical devices that provide facial recognition, voice recognition, GPS and other information to a gaggle of agencies, bureaus, committees and task forces that spend billions to store the time and location of legions of visitors to Washington. At that moment the faces of O'Neil and Ossening were being identified and tagged for several of those agencies. Anyone wanting to know anything about either man would have the image at the speed of light. Those with certain clearances could listen to the conversation.

One of those with such a clearance was wearing headphones and looking at a computer screen in an underground facility in Northern Virginia.

Chapter Fourteen

Sid was old school. He believed that the Internet was the worst thing that had ever happened to the news business, which he refused to call "journalism," believing that once newsmen began to refer to themselves as journalists the backbone went out of the business because reporters now took themselves seriously and began wearing better suits. The Internet made things even worse by making the world wide but shallow, with few areas where depth could be found and turned into a major story with a big audience. Too many outlets and too many crappy people calling themselves "journalists." Cable television made him sick and the great herds of bloggers were even worse.

His believed that reporters first had a duty to make sure no one in high public office got too comfortable. He also believed that nearly every public figure lied about almost anything, sometimes as a matter of habit. And so he had doubts about what the Honorable Mr. Taylor had told Dave.

"This guy is a freshman nobody and he's claiming to have the sole truth, which he's not willing to share with his colleagues. What's wrong with this picture, Dave?"

"What's to lose? I told him I won't use it and I won't. Let's see what he comes up with next."

"What if he's playing you?"

"I assume he is."

"So do I. Why waste your time and mine? The Attorney General has a news conference in two hours. Go cover it and at least you'll have done something to earn your money today. Welcome back."

***

News conferences rarely yield real news. In the absence of a crisis or catastrophe, scheduled news conferences by major public officials are routinely seen as opportunities for the official to issue press release-style statements about how programs are working well, plans are moving ahead, and the nation is in good hands. Dave and most of the reporters he knew did not see scheduled monthly news conferences as anything more than a B-grade story that would be forgotten even while it was on the air.

The AG was the President's pal, a former law partner who had once been a federal prosecutor and had sent a few notorious bad guys to prison, a reputation he still exploited long after the fact and long after he had become very rich by defending the same grade of bad guys he had once hounded.

His news conference on this day was boiler plate self-congratulation about an anti-gang initiative in Chicago which, he claimed, was showing results, despite a sky-high murder rate. The AG had charts, graphs, and reformed gangsters to back up his claim. Broadcast reporters were choosing their sound bites and writing their pieces before the news conferences had ended, assuming it was all standard-issue news gruel.

Dave waited it out, happy to be back among the wretches. Finally, the AG asked if there were questions. Dave raised his hand.

"Mister Attorney General, on another matter, is it true that your office is investigating possible terrorism related to the series of power outages in the Washington region recently?"

The AG glanced at an aide. "Mister Haggard, we are here to discuss a very successful anti-gang program."

"Yes, sir, and we've all heard and taken notes. But about the possible terrorist connection, what is your office doing about it?"

The other reporters stopped what they were doing and looked up. The AG looked down. "I have nothing to say about these reports."

"Is that because the reports are not true or is it because you and others in the government are not making this information public?" Dave kept his tone respectful.

"That is because I have nothing to say. This news conference is over." The AG glared at an aide and walked out.

A wire service reporter walked by Dave and shook his head. "Welcome back, cowboy. I think the terrorist thing has pretty well been put to bed. Just sayin'."

"Seems like it," Dave said, hoping the other reporters shared the wire service guy's opinion. If so, it gave him an open field.

He filed a few bland reports about the AG's news conference, feeling back in the saddle, and went home.

The Cameroonian who was behind the desk in the lobby of his building waved to him and smiled. "You have a letter," he said.

Dave took the letter to his apartment and placed it on the dining table that also served as his desk. He was happy to be back. He made a cup of espresso and stood at the window that overlooked the roof of the parking garage that served the Philadelphia House. He glanced up at the windows of his neighbors, who were not careful about what they did with their blinds open. He saw a woman in her sixties, naked and looking back at him. He waved. She walked away from the window.

He remembered the letter and sat at the table as he opened it. There was no return address, so he assumed it was a solicitation of some kind, probably from someone who wanted to sell him stocks or insurance. He was tempted to throw it out unread. There was no letterhead, only a single sentence in the middle of the page.

"*It is possible to know too much.*" A frowny face was drawn beneath the words.

He turned it over to see if something has been written on the back. Nothing. Dave wondered if it was a joke. He called the desk and the Cameroonian picked up at the first ring.

"This is Dave Haggard. Did you see the person who left the letter for me?"

"It was a man, I think. Thirties, maybe. It was hard to tell. He left it very fast and walked away. He didn't say anything. I'm sorry, sir, I should have asked him who he was."

"No need to apologize. Thank you."

Dave's hands began to shake. He felt a fear that reminded him of other messages that had been dropped off
at the front desk of his apartment building. A rosary from
a murdered priest had been the first, but there had been
others. What could this one mean? He called Inspector
O'Neil and told him he needed to talk. An hour later they
met at a coffee shop at Dupont Circle, two blocks from
Dave's building.

"So, what's new?" O'Neil was relaxed and smiling.

"This." Dave handed the letter to O'Neil, who looked
at it and handed it back.

"And?" O'Neil was still smiling.

"It was dropped off at my apartment building today.
Do you have any idea what it might mean?"

"Why would I know anything about that?"

"You're a cop. You work with clues. This is a clue."

"To what? What are you working on?"

"Give me a break. This obviously has something to
do with the terrorist electric thing."

"I'm sorry but I don't see the word terrorist or power
grid anywhere on this."

Dave was frustrated. "I have a feeling about this, Inspector. There's more to this than you've told me. I questioned the Attorney General about the terrorist angle and
he blew me off. You don't know anything, you say. What
do you know that you're not telling me?"

"Don't get huffy with me, Dave. We have a history
that's not always been positive. I will say this. Yes,
there's more to this than you know, but right now I'm not
going to tell you what it is. You'll have to get that on your
own." O'Neil sat back and crossed his arms.

"I thought we were working together on this. Isn't that why you had me meet Agent Gant?"

"She's not a hundred per cent in on you. She's not much for the media."

"Is that why you're not leveling with me?"

"I am leveling with you. I'm not lying. I'm just not giving you want you want. There's a difference."

Dave considered telling O'Neil about Congressman Taylor but decided it wouldn't get him anything and might even make matters worse, so he kept it to himself and it occurred to him that neither of them trusted the other, a familiar pattern in a relationship that had nearly killed them both.

He called Congressman Taylor, who picked up after one ring. "Let's talk," Taylor said, not bothering to say hello.

Chapter Fifteen

The man who called himself Gutierrez was nervous. He had done all that had been asked of him and was now waiting for further instructions. Days turned into two weeks and there were no communications from whomever was acting as his controller. He switched the lights on and off in one neighborhood after another with no official response from those who supposed to be cowering in the dark. His laptop needed repair, he believed, because it was slow and he often received error messages. Several times the software program that controlled the power grid did not work properly and the lights did not go out or remain out for as long as he wished. He briefly considered that someone had hacked his computer but dismissed the thought because he had been assured that such a thing was not possible, given the program's sophistication and security.

He sat in his hotel room and prayed, cleansed himself, and recited what he remembered of the Quran. He went out only for food and to breathe the air, hating the city and its people and longing for Paradise. *When will I get permission to leave this life?* he wondered.

He was on his knees when they came through the door with their guns and helmets and body armor. They were on him before he could ask what was happening. It was a quick operation, lasting no more than a minute. Later, when a maid entered the room to clean it, she saw nothing of the man who called himself Gutierrez. Not a messy bed. Not a dirty cup. Not a gum wrapper. It was as if he had never been there.

***

Argun Maskhadov watched the black SUV speed away and smiled. He was finished with him. He had been waiting for days for the man to be hauled off. Only a stupid man would believe that he could manipulate the electric grid in the Washington area and not be tracked down and sent to one of their prisons.

The man who called himself Gutierrez would now be known as a prisoner of the United States, nameless, most likely, and caged between interrogations. The poor fellow knew nothing. All of the sophistication of his interrogators would be useless. A man who knows nothing has nothing to offer and so has no value.

Maskhadov had one last task before he was finished with this man. He rented a cargo van and drove to Winchester, Virginia where supplies were hidden. He would move them to a safer place until they were needed, which was less than a week away. Maskhadov believed he was a highly trained professional who would outwit the world's finest. In that he was mistaken. His movements were monitored by a team of former military special operators who were experts at tracking high value targets.

He filled the van with what he needed and drove to a self-storage garage in Frederick, Maryland. He unloaded his cargo and set about assembling the bombs that he would use to make America suffer. He had obtained what he believed were blueprints for Nationals Park and he studied them for weaknesses. He imagined the carnage and it caused him to laugh.

He hated America because the people were comfortable. He also hated Europeans and the Japanese and the newly-rich Chinese and the well-mannered Canadians and all those who spent their lives in safety and comfort. The camps in Ingushetia were not safe and they were not comfortable. Every human quality of dignity was erased in the mud and hatred and humiliation. The strong owned the weak and spent their days in pitiless sport, using the women, even Maskhadov's mother and sisters, as whores and punching bags. Where were the comfortable of the world when his people were living at such a low point? They were enjoying their cocktails and televisions and their luxury cars. They turned their back on the suffering of the world and ordered another round of drinks.

For him, it was not a religious war. It was revenge. Fools like Ikram Ali Ghazali could be made to think that they should long for the death of a martyr, but Maskhadov had other ideas that would bring him comfort, not death. He believed in God but thought He was a jokester who played with his creation in the way a cat toys with a mouse. No, Maskhadov's reward would not involve a dream of virgins in Paradise. It would be sweet revenge.

He assembled his bombs with the materials Ghazali had obtained and left them in the storage garage. He went to the hookah bar and sucked in the bitter smoke, smiling at and despising the young Americans who shared the moment. His cell phone vibrated and he answered. The voice on the other end had been distorted electronically but its message was clear. The mission was to move forward.

Chapter Sixteen

Congressman Taylor met Dave Haggard in a diner at Tysons Corner in Northern Virginia, an area once known for its shopping center but now a growing urban center of office buildings, condos, and Beltway Bandits vacuuming defense and homeland security dollars. Taylor was wearing jeans and a polo shirt and looked rugged and handsome in a magazine-model way. Female diners tried to catch his eye but he ignored them, staring instead at Dave, who was adding sugar to his iced tea.

"How much do you know, Dave?" Taylor's voice was low.

"Off the record?" Dave didn't look up.

"Okay, I'll bite."

"Something is going on that X number of people know something about but aren't talking about. The electric grid thing seems to be some kind of diversion but no one will say or knows what it is. I have a bad feeling that another 9/11 is coming. Am I right?"

Taylor was quiet and glanced around the diner. "We get threats all the time. Some are good and some are just bullshit. This one seems to have some legs. We have the guy who's been turning off the lights but he's either a really good liar or he's a low level hack who's been tossed to the wolves. He claims turning out the lights was sup-posed to scare us and leave us quivering in the dark, or something like that. He's a real fanatic who wants to die a martyr's death so he can get his issue of virgins and live in Paradise and spent all eternity hating infidels. He speaks very good Spanish, by the way. He's Pakistani."

"Who's he working for?" Dave looked up.

"Well, that's the big question, isn't it. He says his handler left messages under rocks, kind of like the old Cold War spy stuff. He says he was ordered to stay away from cell phones and other electronic devices that Ameri-cans spy on. He might be on to something there. He says he doesn't know who he's working for and that he just received orders and carried them out."

"And?"

"He did, even down to gathering material to make a very big bomb out of fertilizer and other things he had no trouble getting his hands on. He took it to Winchester in Virginia and left it, waiting for more instructions."

"What was he going to blow up?"

"Another big question."

"Do you know who his handler is?"

"Not yet."

"So what am I supposed to do with this information?" Dave took a sip of his tea.

"Sit on it. It's all background. If this breaks our way, you'll have a hell of a story. Use it early and you will look like a fool, I promise you."

"What do you want from me?"

"Nothing right how. Later, we can talk." Taylor put a five dollar bill on the table and walked out. A few women watched him leave and offered hopeful smiles.

Dave took his phone out of his shirt pocket and checked to see if the conversation had been recorded. It had. He would play it for Sid.

***

Across the river in an office on the grounds of the old Walter Reed Army Hospital a technician was checking her own recording of the conversation, which would be uploaded to an expanding file that would find its way to O'Neil and Gant by way of another off-the-books Homeland Security office housed several stories underground, a few feet from where Ikram Ali Ghazali was sitting in the dark, praying and wondering when the questioning would begin again.

***

He was left to ponder his situation for twenty-four hours. The darkness was absolute. The cell's floor was polished cement, the walls were painted cinder block. There was a small toilet and sink in a corner. The toilet offered the only relief from the floor and he sat on it for hours, trying to banish the panic that crept into his thoughts. He had no idea where he was or who these people were. They did not identify themselves or offer any reason why he had been seized, although their questions told him they knew who he was and why he was in the United States.

He did not withhold anything. He saw no reason to. His fanaticism did not extend to endless hours of torture. He told himself he would square things with Allah when he entered Paradise, believing that those who had captured him would kill him soon once they believed that he was no longer of value. Allah would understand. He would still die a martyr's death and receive the rewards of those who offered themselves in such a fashion. He had a brief moment of wondering how the virgins he would be given had been chosen. Were they good or bad? Was it a reward or punishment? Most of those he had trained with had no opinion and did not care. A virgin was a virgin. Her fate was not their concern any more than they pondered the dates or other delicacies they were to enjoy.

His reverie was interrupted by the bright lights that flooded the cell as the door was opened. The light hurt his eyes and he was unable to see the men who came for him. He was picked up by his arms and dragged across the floor, through the door, and down a hallway to a small room furnished with two metal chairs, one bolted to the floor.

He was forced to sit in that chair and was shackled behind his back where the shackles were locked, preventing him from moving his arms. He blinked as his eyes adjusted to the light and saw a man sitting in front of him.

"Mr. Ghazali, my name is Peter Taylor and I have a few questions for you." The Congressman had questioned many such men during his second deployment to Afghanistan and was skilled in manipulating them after they had become disoriented by depravation.

Ghazali said nothing. He waited for the torture to begin.

"Please tell me about your childhood, Mr. Ghazali." Taylor smiled and appeared to be friendly. "Were you a happy boy?"

Ghazali said nothing.

"Please excuse my rudeness," Taylor said. "I'll bet you're hungry. May I get you something to eat? We have fruit." He turned to a man at the door and waved his hand. The man walked into the room with a small bowl of grapes, which Taylor offered to Ghazali. He picked one out of the bowl and held it to Ghazali's lips. The man tried to resist but his mouth opened and Taylor placed the grape on his tongue.

Ghazali closed his eyes and slowly chewed the grape, savoring its sweetness. He swallowed the grape and asked for another. Taylor offered each grape slowly, watching Ghazali's eyes follow the fruit from the bowl to his mouth. The Pakistani was like a puppy getting treats, focused only on the next one.

When the bowl was empty Taylor set it on the floor and offered Ghazali a look of compassion. "I'll bet you're wondering what will happen next. Don't worry. We have no plans to harm you. We know you are simply a small piece of the puzzle and that those you work for have thrown you to us. You owe them nothing. Nothing. They do not care what happens to you. They do not care if you ever see your family. They do not care if we kill you or torture you or send you to Guantanamo to waste away for years until you are no longer a man. You owe them nothing. Do you understand me?"

Ghazali believed that this man Taylor was trying to get him to cooperate. He was undecided about it. If they were not going to kill him, his dream of Paradise would not be realized any time soon. What would happen to him in an American prison if he were locked up for years? He had heard the stories and seen the photos of Abu Ghraib in Iraq, where American soldiers tortured and tormented prisoners with dogs and electricity. He needed to find a way out of here so he could carry out a mission that would send him to Paradise.

"What would you like to know?" he asked.

"Tell me about your childhood," Taylor said. Ghazali told his of his birth in a remote area of Pakistan and described how his family had been killed in the conflict that was a way of life in the region. He talked of escapades as a boy, of having been raped by an elder, of working as a porter on mountain trails, and of his discovery of a school where boys were taught the Qu'ran and where they learned to hate the Americans. He talked for hours. His monologue was interrupted by food and water breaks. He was allowed to relieve himself. Taylor was always friendly and repeated that his only goal was to find those who had thrown Ghazali to the Americans. The man warmed to Taylor over the course of two days. On the third day, Taylor took Ghazali for a walk in the warm sunshine and allowed him to pray on a rug facing Mecca.

A day later he took Ghazali to a small garden and sat with him. "What if I offered you freedom? What would you do for me?"

Seventeen

Dave Haggard looked across the table at O'Neil and Gant. The big cop was wearing his official face, the one that cops call "the mask" because there is not a hint of friendliness. It's a power face, one that says I'm in charge. Gant was wearing her F.B.I. face, the one that says you can trust me. Someone at Quantico had decided that 'trust me' was better than 'fear me', at least under some circumstances. Dave knew that he was being played or even interrogated.

"To what do I owe this free cup of coffee?" he said.

"We just want to know what you've learned from your sources," O'Neil responded, sitting back with is arms crossed.

"What sources? You're my sources and you don't seem to know much of anything."

"I didn't say we didn't know anything, Dave. I said we can't tell you what we know."

Gant had the look of a friendly fourth grade teacher, all supportive and smiley. "We need to work together. We can't be your sources, officially at least. This could be serious, Dave. We need your help. If you know something, tell us. It could make a difference."

Dave almost laughed out loud. "I thought you two worked in dead-end jobs where you pushed paper and went to useless meetings. Now you're suggesting that you're the dynamic duo?"

"Don't be an asshole, Dave." O'Neil's face revealed anger but Dave thought it looked contrived.

"Let's be clear. You're playing me. I know it. You know it. Let's cut the crap." Dave looked at both of them.

"Have you ever asked yourself why people like us give information to people like you?" O'Neil was not smiling.

"Tit for tat," Dave replied. "You give and you get."

"What do we get?" Gant was smirking.

"This town is full of people offering everything they know for one reason or another. How do I know what you two are getting out of this? Wait! You're not getting any-thing because you're not giving anything." Dave sat back and waited for one of them to confirm what he had just said.

"Not true, Dave." O'Neil leaned forward with a seri-ous cop expression that had been used on street punks in back rooms.

"How so?"

"We gave you the terrorist angle before you had any idea it was more than another storm-related outage, to use the media term for the lights going out."

"And that appears to be a quickly dying story."

Gant and O'Neil exchanged smirks. "Jesus, this is a waste of time," Gant whispered.

"Let's begin again," O'Neil said. "What are you hearing?"

***

While Dave, Gant and O'Neil were doing the Washington source dance at a coffee shop downtown, Argun Maskhadov was buying tickets for the Nationals game against Milwaukee. He used a ticket machine outside the stadium and had no preference in seats, taking the first option that came to him, an outfield seat with a clear view of home plate and the expensive seats behind it. He wandered through the mezzanine, grabbing a crab cake sandwich and a soft drink, cursing at the cost, twenty-one dollars. "This is robbery!" he shouted at the woman behind the counter.

"You don't havta eat it, hon," she said. "Next."

Eating crab is halal, he was told, because the Prophet has said it is permissible to eat all things from the sea. Some of his Chechen friends argued that it was never permissible to eat shellfish.

"No," he told them, "Only Jews do not eat shellfish." And so he enjoyed the crab cake sandwich and observed others as they watched batting practice and bought trinkets as souvenirs.

Maskhadov walked to the upper decks and looked down at the field. He tried to imagine a conflagration of explosions, fire, and panic as a crowd of infidels perished in an act of retribution. He felt sick to his stomach and wondered if it was the height or something else. He did not want to consider what that something else might be for fear it would shake his resolve to do this deed.

He found his seat as the first batter approached the plate. He had learned to like baseball and appreciated its pace and strategies. He marveled at how fast the ball moved from the pitcher's hand to the catcher's mitt. How can anyone hit such a moving object? he wondered. The batter struck out and the next man approached the plate. Maskhadov lost himself in the game and was surprised when the seventh inning stretch had everyone standing and singing *Take Me Out To The Ballgame.* The Nationals were ahead by three runs at the point and he saw no reason to stay, so he walked out through the center field gate, bumping into Johnny Holliday, who was preparing for his post-game television show. Holliday was a fixture in the Washington sports scene and his face was known to even casual followers. To Nationals fans, Holliday was as famous as any of the players.

"Excuse me," Maskhadov said, stopping to help Holliday pick up some papers.

"No problem," Holliday replied. "Enjoying the game?" He offered his hand and the two men shook. He smiled and patted Maskhadov on the shoulder.

"Very much, thank you."

The two men went to their own destinations. Maskhadov briefly thought of going back to ask for Holliday's autograph but thought it risky should Holliday remember him. Instead, he took Metro to Chinatown, changed to the Red Line, and took the train to Shady Grove, the end of the line, where he had parked a rental car. By midnight he was in Frederick, smoking from the hookah, and asking himself why his hands were shaking.

Chapter Eighteen

Ikram Ali Ghazali spent the night on a comfortable mattress between soft sheets. The room was cool. In the dark it was easy to forget that the walls were concrete painted a sickly green and there were no windows to the outside. He was given a prayer rug and told which of the green walls faced Mecca. He was allowed to wash himself from a basin of clear water. He was presented with a Qur'an to read before the lights went out. He was treated with great respect which, despite himself, he found satisfying, even though he knew it was all part of the game to get him to cooperate in their scheme.

He lay beneath the soft sheet and felt at peace. They were right, he acknowledged. He had been thrown to the wolves. The power grid plan was only a ruse, a way to call attention away from their real plan and he was nothing more than a sacrifice. He had killed a man for nothing. The traitor, the man named Rodell Clark, had been no more important than an insect to be squashed. All of the schemes to control the power grid were only child's games and Clark had been expendable.

He moved to the prayer rug and wept as he recited the verse:

...Nor take life - which Allah has made sacred - except for just cause. And if anyone is slain wrongfully, we have given his heir authority (to demand retaliation or to forgive): but let him not exceed bounds in the matter of taking life, for he is helped (by the Law)"

Ghazali knew this killing was not just cause and Clark was slain wrongfully. How to atone? What could he offer Clark's heir? The head of the man who caused this unjust killing? To do that he must cooperate with this man Taylor and his kind. What that just? The man Clark was an infidel and his killing was justified if only for that. But he was in a nest of infidels and the killing of one without a clear purpose was a threat to his eternity in Paradise. To cooperate was also a threat. Would it make him a traitor? He prayed for guidance, went back to his bed, and slept.

A dream came to him. A man on a white horse rode to him and raised a sword, which brought a shower of fire from the sky. Thousands of souls screamed to Paradise for salvation but there was no answer. Ghazali was caught in the screams and felt himself being pulled into the fire, but there was no heat, only anguish. The man on the horse had no flesh on his face but his eyes were black and knowing. He raised the sword and swung it at Ghazali's neck. He awoke with a scream and had trouble breathing. He trembled as he tried to shake off the dream and its terrible images. He did not sleep again that night. In the morning he told Taylor he would cooperate and help him find the man who had unjustly caused the death of the man named Clark.

***

Taylor spent two days interrogating Ghazali. He and others on a team of special operators were experts at keeping their subjects at the edge of control. Ghazali would spill his guts about one thing only to be harshly interrogated about something that had no importance, such as the value of coffee over tea or whether sandals were better for the feet than sneakers.

"Tell me again about the madrasa," Taylor said. "What time in the morning did you begin your studies. How long did it take you to memorize each passage? Did you desire to be with girls while you were praying?" The questions came very fast and Ghazali had trouble keeping up. Taylor suddenly went quiet at times, leaving Ghazali disoriented. There were no windows in the room and he could not tell whether it was day or night.

On the third day Taylor called Dave Haggard and arranged a meeting at his office on Capitol Hill. "Here's the deal," Taylor said. "We got us a goat. We turned him and he's going to be working for us. Can I trust you?"

"You know what I'm going to say, so whether you can trust me is up to you."

"Screw me and you will never know peace. Understood?"

"What's in it for you?" Dave asked. He wondered what sort of game was being played.

"The American people are often told that terrorists are plotting against us. Nothing ever happens so some people think we just bullshit everybody to get money for guns and war toys. This is real. There is a plot to do something very bad. You can have the story and be on the inside but the deal is you keep your mouth shut, I mean shut, until I give the go signal. Deal?"

"So you want me to be a fly on the wall as this plays out and then put the story out."

"Something like that."

"You know I will have to tell my boss." Dave was already thinking of Sid's reaction.

"That's your problem. He has a solid reputation even if he's kind of a dinosaur. He'll have to keep it quiet just like you and I have to insist that you keep the loop at two. No briefing the board of directors or editors or any of that. You and your boss. No more."

"Deal."

***

Taylor spent an hour briefing Dave on Ghazali and Argun Maskhadov, who was being observed by a team of professionals who were hoping that Maskhadov would lead them to his superiors.

"So, this is how it's done?" Dave asked.

"What was it that the politician said? There are known knowns and known unknowns and unknown unknowns? Something like that. We never know what we don't know. The guys who are working on this have lots of experience in very dangerous places but ain't over till it's over. What I want to get out there whenever this ends is that bad people want to do very bad things and despite the politicians who play with themselves all day there are people who are in the fight." Taylor's hands were trembling and he made fists and pounded them on the table. "Goddam it!"

"So what's next?" Dave wondered if Taylor was going to start smashing the furniture.

"We let this guy Ghazali loose and see what happens."

"What if he runs?"

"He won't run and if he does he won't get far."

"Let me ask you this. How long was he in the country before you picked him up?"

"What difference does that make?"

"How long?"

"We picked him up after he got sloppy with the power outages. Our guys are very good."

"Not that good. He got into the country and made mischief before you got him. How do you know he's not good enough to escape your little cage?"

"He won't." Taylor's face was firm but Dave saw some doubt in his eyes.

"If this heads south and he takes off and he does something bad it will be part of my story."

"Won't happen." Taylor stood and waved Dave to the door. "Stay by your phone."

Nineteen

Ghazali was driven in a plain American-made sedan to a bus stop on 16th Street Northwest where the door was opened and he was ordered to get out. In his pocket was five-thousand dollars in cash, mostly twenties with some fifties in the mix. He was handed a Metro card with a value of fifty dollars. There were two other men in the car and neither spoke. Once Ghazali was out, the car sped away and he was left alone in the dark. He was two blocks south of Columbia Road and he caught the scent of the restaurants that offered Third-World dishes from Latin America to Southwest Asia. He had no fixed schedule, so he walked up to Columbia and headed west to the sounds of Latin music and happy people on the sidewalks.

He found a small storefront restaurant where a Somali woman waved him inside and pointed to a table near the window. He ordered okra stew and roasted goat encrusted with cumin, nutmeg, cinnamon and garlic and savored the delicacy of the meal, washed down with spiced tea. He felt at peace, even with the knowledge that somewhere nearby were men who were watching him. He had been trained for such moments and he called upon the patience that would be needed in the days ahead.

He paid in cash and walked through the crowds in what was a mostly Hispanic neighborhood, listening to the music and allowing himself a moment of contentment. He was, at that moment, a happy man who believed he was in control of his life. His time in the cell had given him an appreciation of the freedom he had to eat what he chose and walk where he wished.

He found a Cuban coffee shop and sat at a table where three other men were sipping strong coffee.

"¿puedo" *May I*

"Si, por favor." *Yes, please*. One of the men smiled and waved at the seat Ghazali already occupied.

"Soy Gutiérrez." *I am Gutierrez.* Ghazali offered his hand.

"Estoy Sánchez y este es Garza." *I am Sanchez and this is Garza.* Smiles all around.

"Soy nuevo aquí." *I am new here.* Ghazali, now back to calling himself Gutierrez, offered a shy face.

"Todos somos nuevos aquí, mi amigo." *We are all new here*. Garza laughed.

And so the evening passed, with the once-again Gutierrez sharing stories with his new friends while unseen eyes watched and took notes. Within twenty-four hours the new friends would be on a plane to Honduras, unaware that certain powers in America had no tolerance for anyone who would be a companion to the man who called himself Gutierrez.

***

Argun Maskhadov had been trained by those who not only had honed their hatred to a fine and lethal point, but were also experts in the dark arts of espionage and killing. Suicide vests were not on the agendas of these men, they were too valuable to be blown up on a public street. That was for the lesser ones whose martyrdom added energy to the cause. His trainers had been to the schools of the very best, some even by the CIA or Chinese Ministry of State Security or Russia's GRU. One had been trained in North Korea where those who failed to complete the course were executed by those who had.

Maskhadov knew he was being tailed and that told him a great deal. They knew who he was and therefore he assumed they knew why he was here. Ghazali! he thought. A traitor! But he rejected that answer because it made no sense. Ghazali did not know who he was. Ghazali was a fool. No, it was not likely that those who tailed him were following a trail from the Pakistani. They were good, he had to admit. But not good enough. They did not conceal themselves well and were now prey.

He drank his coffee and planned his moves, like a chess master, knowing that one move will provoke an opponent into a predictable position from which he can be taken. What bait did he have? He opened a small notebook and wrote in two columns, one for his strengths, the other for the strengths of his opponents. He made two more columns for weaknesses. He stared at the paper and a plan came to him. He would need access to his explosives but he didn't want to risk losing his supply if he were overpowered in an unexpected move on their part. No, he would need another source.

He drove to the town of Cumberland in the mountains of western Maryland and found a workingman's bar where men with callused hands were throwing down beer and whiskey. He bought a round and asked if construction jobs were available. He told the men he met that he was a Russian who had done security jobs for the Americans in Afghanistan and needed work now that the war was winding down. The men he met were nice if not friendly and they thanked him for helping the United States. A man who appeared to be quite drunk told him that a road crew was needed to cut a new road through the mountains in Garrett County, in far western Maryland, The pay was good but the work was brutal. He thanked the man, bought another round for his new friends, and drove west.

He found the job site by following the signs warning drivers to turn off their cell phones to prevent accidental explosions. He waited until dark when the work crew left the site in the hands of a minimum wage security guard who sat in his car and smoked a joint before nodding off. An hour later Maskhadov was headed east with what he needed.

Chapter Twenty

Dave Haggard woke to the sound of his phone, a distinct dobro riff that called to mind his East Tennessee upbringing. He had trouble shaking off his sleep, more of a stupor, and the phone went to voice message before he could answer. He rolled onto his back and stared at the ceiling, reminding himself again that he needed to tell the building management that water from the apartment above was staining the paint.

His mouth was dry and his head was pounding, sure signs that he had emptied another bottle of fine Tennessee whiskey. "I'm a goddam drunk," he said out loud, hoping it would motivate him to do something. What, he didn't know. Ever since he'd been shot in the spring he had been hiding his fears in booze, a legacy of his stepfather, who had spent the last twenty years of his life drinking himself to death.

He swung his legs over the bed and managed to stand up, wobbling to the kitchen, where he fixed himself a cup of espresso. He downed it in one gulp, burning his mouth, and headed for the bathroom where he stepped into a cold shower and howled as his body slowly came to life. It was thirty minutes before he felt human and another hour before he could muster the energy to check his phone. There were three messages. One from Congressman Taylor. One from Sid. One from Elena.

Elena! He loved her and hated the relationship. She was a temporary fix to his loneliness, like the whiskey, but he could not bring himself to commit to her. She needed someone to be a partner and share her life. He liked the idea that she was beautiful and offered him sex. He could not be there to listen to her fears and dreams.

He played the messages. Taylor wanted to meet. Sid wanted him to cover the Attorney General's weekly news conference. Elena's message was short. She had left a letter at the desk and he should read it. Goodbye.

He felt relieved. Maybe this time it really was goodbye. Over. They would never see each other again. He would lose the sex but gain freedom from what she needed. He admitted to himself that she was the grownup in the relationship. He had spent the summer at the beach with her, listening to her scoldings about his drinking and brooding. He wondered how she had put up with him. At times, he couldn't stand himself and it amazed him that Elena and others could. Well, now, he knew. She couldn't either. He would read the letter later.

He called Taylor and arranged to meet him at a Capitol Hill watering hole popular with journalists and members of Congress. The meeting would appear to be just another drink between a reporter and a junior member of the House. No one would notice. Eyes would be on whoever was drinking with senior Members.

Sid was more of a problem. The AG's news conference was to start in fifteen minutes. It was nine blocks from his condo. He called Sid.

"I overslept," he said by way of introduction.

"Get your ass down there," Sid growled, hanging up.

***

The Attorney General was being introduced as Dave walked into the briefing room and plugged his smartphone into a mult-box that fed audio to the broadcasters in attendance. He opened his notebook and tried to act interested, longing to close his eyes and drift away until his head cleared. The AG's news conference was boilerplate media stuff, an announcement of a new Justice Department initiative to raise awareness about gun violence, the release of a new report showing the Department was doing a fine job tracking down cyber criminals, and a preliminary report showing that auto thefts nationwide were trending down. Any questions?

"Yes." Dave raised his hand. "Is there anything new on the recent Washington area power outages and the link to terrorism?"

"We know of no such link." The AG's response was curt and he turned away to call upon a reporter in the back, who wanted to know more about the auto thefts. Two more questions and the AG left the briefing without a glance at Dave or anyone else.

***

He went to Now News and filed a couple of standard-issue reports for the feeds to the stations around the country and knocked on Sid's door.

"I have a meeting with Taylor tonight."

"Have you ever heard of a snipe hunt?" Sid asked.

"Sure. It's where a group of guys take an unsuspecting man out to the woods at night for what he's told is a snipe hunt. They give him a sack and tell him to hold it open while they drive the snipe his way so he can catch it in the bag. Then they leave. That's where the phrase holding the bag comes from."

"Do you think you're holding the bag on this? Did it occur to you that Taylor and the others are just playing you to keep you away from what's really going on here?"

"Why would they do that?"

"My god! Did you just get off the boat? How long have you been working in this city? Look up lying bullshit artists in the dictionary and there's a picture of the Capitol. We can sit on this for now but tell Taylor that unless we get something more concrete than his spy novel meetings we're out of this game. And O'Neil and whatsername, the F.B.I. lady, they're even worse. Everybody's got you tied up in some kind of secret society. This stinks, Dave."

"Yeah, it's tiring," Dave said. "I was hoodwinked at a carnival once by a guy who kept telling me I was close to the big prize, but I ran out of money just short of the win. You think it's the same game here?"

"How does it feel inside?"

"I get your meaning. I'll call you tonight."

***

Dave went back to his condo and retrieved Elena's letter from the front desk. It was sealed in an envelope that was scented with her perfume. It aroused him and he allowed himself a fantasy that the letter was an erotic invitation. It was written in her elegant Catholic school cursive and the nuns would have been proud of her penmanship.

Dear Dave, it began. Those were the last friendly words. She reminded him that she had stuck with him even though she had been nearly murdered by a homicidal priest he was reporting on. She reminded him that she had stuck with him after he had been shot chasing a story about a hit man and a corrupt member of Congress. She had nursed him and cared for him. He had given back only his selfishness and obsession with his work. He read to the end and laughed at her use of curse words, which he found endearing. *You are a prick and an asshole and a motherfucker and I hope you never get laid again in your life.*

The last line was the saddest of all. He would miss her dirty talk. He fell asleep and dreamed that Elena was floating in his apartment, smiling and beaconing to him. In the dream he could not move. He awoke to the knowledge that her letter was her way of calling him to her. She was asking, again, for him to pursue her and beg for her forgiveness. He showered and went to meet Taylor.

Twenty-One

Rayburn's Bar was a nod to the late Sam Rayburn, the legendary Speaker of the House in the mid Twentieth Century. Rayburn was from Texas, although he was born in Roane County, Tennessee, the birthplace of Dave Haggard. Unlike Dave, Rayburn was a natural-born deal maker. The House's newest and grandest office building is named after him. None of that mattered to those who gathered Rayburn's Bar to swap rumors and gossip about who was doing what to whom in the House and Senate.

The place was a warren of small tables close together, guarded by men and women in blue or gray suits, white shirts, and red ties. The standard uniform in Washington. Boozy conversations over expensive drinks and trendy snacks provided the fuel for the chattering classes who gathered in Congressional hallways, cable television studios, or lobbying firms. Body language was read like tea leaves for hints of shifts in political winds or, more important, funding, the basic life force in the capital.

Congressman Taylor was at the bar, chatting with an attractive, earnest-faced young woman who seemed to be entranced by the Member who bought her a drink. He was looking quite full of himself and gazed at the woman in the way a lion appraises a careless gazelle.

Dave made his way through the room and tapped Taylor on the shoulder. "Hello, Congressman. I hope I'm not interrupting anything." The woman looked annoyed.

"Not at all, at least not yet," Taylor said. "May I introduce Wendy. Wendy, this is Dave Haggard. He's a reporter. The one who got shot a few months ago."

"Nice to meet you," Wendy said. "We were having a conversation." She glanced at Taylor with a look that told him to get rid of Dave.

"Sorry, Wendy, we have something to discuss. Maybe I'll see you here again." He pulled Dave to a table as Wendy appeared to be on the verge of tears.

"Nice looking," Dave said. A waiter came by and they ordered craft beer.

"Shooting fish in a barrel," Taylor said. "They see the suit and the lapel pin that Members wear and they can't keep their pants on."

"Must be nice."

"It can get tiring. I don't mean that in a physical sense." Taylor had a weary expression.

"What's up?"

"We have a small problem. We've lost this guy Maskhadov. He's better than we thought he was and he's loose. We're hoping the Pakistani will help us pick up his trail."

"Ghazali? He's loose too?"

"I told you, we're using him as a goat, as bait. He's convinced Maskhadov threw him to the wolves and we've got him out trying to lure him in. We need to catch him doing more than driving around. We think he's plotting a big event but we need to be on him."

"How'd you lose him?"

"How do you lose anyone? One minute he's there, the next he's not."

"Why are you telling me?"

"Like I said, we want you in the loop when this goes down. You'll have a hell of a story."

"I need to have something here. I need to have something I can report."

"One week, Dave. Stick with this for one week."

"Why a week?"

"You'll see." Taylor's cell phone buzzed. He looked at it and put it to his ear. "Shit!" His shoulders sagged and he turned to Dave. "Ghazali's gone, too."

"I thought you guys were pros." Dave stared at Taylor and wondered if the whole affair was nothing more than a farce.

"We are. As it turns out, so are they. We should have seen that this was too easy." Taylor looked around like a man hoping a miracle would walk through the door. What he saw was just more Washington hot air rising from the mouths of the chattering class. No solutions there.

"I have to go," he said. "Not a word about this. We're in lockdown on all of this until further notice." He pushed his way through the crowd and shoved his way past a smiling young woman who was tapping on his shoulder, hoping for a conversation.

***

The man who again called himself Gutierrez was at that moment riding Metro to the Shady Grove station. He had no plan other than separating himself from his tail. He wore a Washington baseball cap, a hoodie pulled up over his head and large sunglasses. He looked like any other young man with an attitude riding the Red Line. Several other young men were similarly dressed and sported sunglasses in the darkness.

His immediate challenge was to grab his bag at the hotel where he had been staying. The bag contained the cash he would need to survive until the end, whenever it came. He had stashed it in the hotel's garage on a support beam in the back of the lower level, where the chance that it would be discovered was very low. He had to retrieve it before dawn. His mind went over the possibilities. Those who were pursing him may already be scouring the hotel for any sign of him. How long would it take for them to organize a search? Hours? Minutes?

He got off at Shady Grove and caught a bus to Rockville, back in the direction of D.C. He changed busses several times until he found himself downtown within sight of his hotel. There was one obvious security vehicle in front, but no other sign of them. The entrance to the garage was on 15th Street Northwest, a busy thoroughfare even at midnight. It was not a neighborhood of gangsta dress, so he ditched the hoodie and sunglasses and pulled the cap down low on his face. He knew security cameras were recording images of everyone in the garage . He would have to move fast. He slipped down the ramp past the parking card machines and crawled along the walls behind the vehicles that were parked on the first level. He ran down the ramp to the second level and repeated his crawl along the wall behind the cars. Hotel party goers and guests either didn't see him or paid no attention. It didn't matter. He would never be there again.

He ran down to the third level, found his bag where he had stashed it, checked to see if it had been tampered with, and took the stairs to a street level exit. He had a thought that made him laugh and ran up to Pennsylvania Avenue, where he turned left toward the White House, a block away. He strolled up to the fence and waved. He shook hands with a startled uninformed Secret Service officer, telling the man, "It's great to be in America, amigo!" The officer smiled and stood back as the man who called himself Gutierrez jogged toward 17th Street.

Two hours later he was in a cheap motel in Hyattsville, Maryland across the line in Prince Georges County, counting his cash. The motel was a by-the-week dump that catered to the down and out. It did not take credit cards or checks. The room was musty and the sheets were stained, but the water was hot and he was alone, so, for the moment, he was content. He prayed and cleansed himself, climbed into the musty bed, and slipped into a peaceful sleep.

***

By dawn Taylor, Ossening, O'Neil and Gant were reviewing the videos, each in their spaces. Only Taylor knew what the images meant. The others were several steps behind and it would be days before they caught up. By then, the game would be changed.

Chapter Twenty-Two

Argun Maskhadov stared at his face in the mirror and saw a man who had dead eyes. He tried to remember a time in his life when he was happy. He could not. The men he had known as a boy were all hard and mean and tempered by hatred. The men who sat and told stories believed that God had chosen Chechens to suffer and, in the bargain, to become strong enough to right the wrongs of the world, which were many. The West was a nest of Satan's agents. Christians were led astray by the early Church and were no longer to be trusted with the message of the prophet Jesus. These so-called Christians had spent centuries spreading slaughter and suffering in the name of their Christ. They were infidels who's sins were to be expiated through endless pain and death. Maskhadov's family lived in hunger, misery and fear and only the promise of death to the West made life bearable. Only death to Russia was sweeter. The Russian Christian church had been the most evil, in the eyes of those whom Maskhadov admired.

Now, his time had come. He again looked at his face and smiled. He would shave his beard and reveal his face for the first time since Allah Most Merciful had granted him a thick, black blanket over his cheeks, chin and neck.

In his heart he was not a devout man. He did not pray daily. He did not observe Ramadan. He did not own a prayer rug. He could not recite great passages of the Quran. But he had kept his face covered in his beard and had worn the taqiyah, a skull cap, during his stays in Pakistan and Iran, where he was trained.

His time of pride would come again but now it was time for action. He knew he was no martyr and he was not a volunteer to be blown into a pink cloud of blood and brains. He would survive. He must be smarter than his foe. He had already outwitted them by escaping their surveillance and now he would do it again.

He applied thick soapy foam to his face and moved the razor. Slowly a thin, scarred face emerged. His cheeks were hollow. His chin was pointed. His head appeared smaller and less sinister. He stared at the new face in the mirror. Only the eyes were the same. The places where his beard had grown were lighter than his nose and forehead. He must sit in the sun to hide the outline of the beard. He must have his hair cut into a style consistent with who he wanted to be. A professional, perhaps, someone who parts his hair and puts on the air of a man who works in an office and wears suits as a matter of course.

He showered and dressed into khaki trousers and a polo shirt. He went to a mall and purchased an inexpensive suit, two dress shirts, two ties, socks and black dress shoes. He went to a chain hair-styling shop and told the Vietnamese woman who worked there that he wanted a businessman's haircut. When she was finished he looked like every other man who walked out of the place. He returned to his room and changed into his new clothes. He felt ridiculous. He imagined the laughs he would receive from his old friends in the refugee camp. He found it unimaginable that anyone would believe he was an American businessman.

He drove to the Shady Grove Metro station and purchased a ticket that would take him to downtown Washington. He got off at Metro Center and walked up 12th Street Northwest to K Street, turned left, and assumed the quick pace of the others on the sidewalk, men and women who worked at lobbying firms or law offices and saw themselves as orchids in a world of dandelions. No one gave him a second glance. They were too wrapped in their own self-importance to notice the man in the cheap suit.

He was elated. He found a restaurant with outdoor tables and ordered dinner, studying the other men and mimicking their manners. He held his fork as they held theirs. He gave his face the expression they offered. He felt like an actor on a stage. He found that he enjoyed the experience and decided to spend a few days being this new man just for the fun of it.

It was Friday, a day of prayer for the faithful. The men prayed at the Mosque in the early afternoon, then went about their business. At sunset those who had made this mission possible would leave him a message and they expected a progress report. His instructions were simple. A plus sign if the mission was moving ahead and a minus sign if it was not. He wrote a plus sign on a small piece of paper and walked into a park at 14th and K. There were benches along the walkway that were shaded by tall trees. He found the proper bench, sat, and retrieved a small piece of paper that was folded into a tight square. He inserted his own message and left.

He took the Red Line back to the Shady Grove station and waited until the passengers thinned at the last stop in D.C., then he opened his message. It was short. Ghazali was free. He was instructed to find him.

***

Ghazali, aka Gutierrez, was immersed in his Mexican cover in a small apartment in Adams Morgan, just off Columbia Road. There were five people in the apartment, three men and two women. The women were in the kitchen and the men were sitting on two broken down sofas that did not match and had the look of something donated by a charity, which they were. Across the dirty linoleum floor a large television displayed images of young women in scanty bathing suits gyrating to Latin music. The two men the one known at Gutierrez had come to see were wearing new cowboy boots with pointed toes, new Levis, and large straw cowboy hats. They stared at the images of the young women with serious, studious faces, as though they were examining something important.

One of the men was in his fifties. The other was his son by a woman he had kept while he was married to one of the women in the kitchen, who treated the young man as her own.

"Así, mi amigo, ¿qué puedo hacer por ti?" *So, my friend, what can I do for you?* The older man said, not moving his gaze from the television.

"Estoy en peligro. Necesito protegerme." *I am in danger and I must protect myself.* The man known as Gutierrez tried to appear humble.

"Yo no soy un agente de policía." *I am not a police officer.* The man removed his gaze from the images of dancing women and looked at Gutierrez. "Tal vez debería llamar al 911." *Perhaps you should call 911.*

"Es importante que yo me ocupo de esto yo mismo." *It is important that I take care of this myself.*

The man gave Gutierrez a long stare. " Lo que usted necesita le costará mil dólares. Voy a tirar en una caja de balas." *What you require will cost you one thousand dollars. I will throw in one box of bullets.* He waited for Gutierrez reaction. "Ningún crédito. *Cash.* Si se remonta a me voy a convertir este asunto en manos de mis amigos de la MS-13. Ellos se ocuparán de usted de una manera que no te gustará." *No credit. Cash. If it is traced back to me I will turn this matter over to my friends at MS-13. They will deal with you in a manner you will not like.*

MS-13 is one of Central America's most vicious and ruthless gangs. They had been building their strength and influence in the Washington area's Hispanic community and members had been convicted of murders and mutilations of anyone who challenged them. For many Hispanics, the mere mention of MS-13 was terrifying.

"No habrá necesidad de involucrar a nadie más." *There will be no need to involve anyone else.*

The older man nodded to his son, who went to another room and returned with a cardboard box. The younger man stepped in front of Gutierrez and opened the box, displaying a handgun in a cotton sock and a box of nine millimeter shells.

"Beretta. Fue robado de la base militar donde los reservistas entrenan. Será detectable pero no está relacionado con un crimen en esta ciudad." *Beretta. It was stolen from an Army base where reservists train. It will be traceable but it is not linked to a crime in this city.*

Gutierrez knew that he could probably pick up the same Beretta at a gun store for half the price but that was not an option. He gave the man ten one-hundred dollar bills. He took the handgun from the box and slipped it into the waistband of his pants. He put the shells in a pocket of the hoody, shook hands with the men, and walked out onto Columbia Road. It took him nearly an hour to find a spot in Rock Creek Park to spend the night.

Chapter Twenty-Three

The image of the man who called himself Gutierrez shaking hands with a uniformed Secret Service officer in front of the White House was cause for high-fives in offices where it was believed that so-called special operators were unduly worshipped within the intelligence community. This man, this Ghazali-Gutierrez fellow, had slipped away from those who claimed to be highly trained and had the moxie to give them the finger as he left. Those who saw the photo were a small but plugged-in bunch who normally spent their days reviewing images, videos, documents and files that were boring to the extreme and involved reports of one person on one list who made a call to another person on another list.

The post 9/11 policy of "sharing" information had produced mountains of information that mostly added up to nothing. Occasionally, something of importance came over the transom and very rarely something that caused the foundations of the republic to shake. This case was shaping up to be one of those. It was clear that this man, whoever he was, was as good as our guys and maybe even better, given the current score, or so it was said among certain agents.

O'Neil and Gant watched the video a dozen times. O'Neil laughed each time. Gant did not see the humor in it and shouted "goddam it!" each time she watched.

"Son of a bitch is good," O'Neil said, pointing to the screen.

"There are two ways to look at it," Gant said. "Either he's good or we're bad. My money is on some son of a bitch hanging for this."

"Who's supposed to be watching him?" O'Neil asked.

"Some super troopers who operate of a black operation in Fairfax County. My guess is something out of N.S.A. These days, who knows? Could be freelancers or contractors."

The phone rang. It was Ossening at the F.B.I.

"So, how are J. Edgar Hoover's boys this morning?" O'Neil said by way of greeting.

"He's dead. Long time now. It was in all the papers. You looking at what I'm looking at?"

"Several times," O'Neil said.

"Thoughts?"

"Hey, I'm just a paper pusher. I thought you heroes of the republic were on the case."

"I've got my own papers to move around. What are you hearing?"

"Nothing but noise."

"Me, too. Coffee?"

"I'll bring Gant. You two can swap Quantico stories."

"Fifteen minutes. Navy Memorial."

The three of them sat on the steps of the amphitheater and watched tourists take pictures of each other. A group of Chinese tourists got off a bus, spent five minutes snapping photos on their phones, and returned to the bus, having checked another Washington attraction off the list. A family of five with the wholesome look of the Midwest smiled and allowed themselves to be amazed at everything in their Nation's Capital, offering "wows" to each other after every photo.

"Were you ever like that?" Ossening asked, pointing to the Midwesterners.

"Like what?" Gant replied.

"You know, all wide-eyed and patriotic."

"Still am," she said. It was no joke.

"Aren't you a bit cynical by now, with all you know about how it really works?"

"How does it work?" She glared at him.

Ossening ignored her and turned his attention to O'Neil. "So, nothing new in your inbox?"

"Same old same old," O'Neil said.

"I have a theory," Ossening said. "I think your pal Dave Haggard is drinking from lots of wells on this. He knows more than we know. The question is who else is he talking to."

"He's not talking," O'Neil said.

"Because he's not getting anything in return," Ossening said.

"You two spend a lot of your time talking about this guy. Why do you think a reporter is important?" Gant had a look of despair.

"Reporters in this city are kind of like transfer points on Metro. It's how you get form one point to another," Ossening said. "Think of them as jumper cables."

"I take it you flunked your metaphor class," Gant said, turning her face to the sun.

"You get my meaning," Ossening said.

"Sort of. Anyway, what do we have to offer him? He's not accepting promises as payment, he made that clear, and he's not putting anything on the table." Gant's voice was trailing off as though she was already out of the conversation.

"I might have something," Ossening said. "There's a Congressman, a guy named Taylor, who's got a background in this stuff. Let me see if I can find a connection to Haggard. Maybe these two guys are friendly. It's worth a shot."

"Whiskey or bullet?" O'Neil said.

"Both," Ossening said, standing and walking away without another word.

***

Twenty-four hours later Ossening's contacts in the F.B.I. paid off. He debated whether to share the information with O'Neil and Gant. Gant was on the outs with the Bureau and was serving penance in her current assignment. O'Neil was a loose cannon whose own people wanted him exiled. But then, he had to admit, he was not on a personal voyage to the top of the Hoover Building, either.

He waited forty eight hours to call O'Neil.

Chapter Twenty-Four

Dave Haggard's drinking had become a problem for Sid. His ace reporter was hung over and late most mornings and he had been late to a few news conferences, not that it mattered. Dave had friends who would fill him in and even share audio with him if he missed a key soundbite. But Dave was definitely headed down. Sid had seen a sad number of talented reporters drink themselves out of the news business. He called Dave in for a talk and, as usual, Dave sulked as he sat in front of Sid's desk.

"You're looking kind of ragged today," Sid said by way of opening.

"You're not so bad yourself," Dave said, staring at the floor.

"I'm not much for the touchy feely stuff, Dave. I'll get right to it. Pull yourself together. Get a handle on the drinking and go looking for your self-respect. You can't brood like some pissed-off nine year old."

"I can handle it," Dave said. His eyes were bloodshot and the scent of alcohol drifted over Sid's desk in a foul cloud.

"Yeah, I see how you can handle it. What is it? Elena? She says you two are finished. That right?"

"Pretty much, yup."

"Is that why you're having this boozy pity party?"

"I like to relax in the evenings."

"That's what you call it, relaxing?" Sid leaned forward with his elbows on his desk. "I call it pretty shitty behavior. You're better than this, Dave. If you're not dry by the end of the week I'm shipping you off to rehab. If you won't go, you're out of a job. I don't have any use for a drunk."

"You can't fire me. I'm the best you've got." Dave raised his head and looked at Sid.

"Not now you're not. You're just another fuckup on the payroll."

"Thanks for your support." Dave was whining and he knew it.

"Enough with the alcoholic bullshit. Get yourself together or get out."

Dave sulked as he went into the newsroom, grabbed his coat, and took a cab back to his apartment, where he downed a fifth of whiskey and passed out.

***

F.B.I. agents who are selected for special training can penetrate even the most secure buildings. During the Cold War they routinely entered the Soviet Embassy and planted listening devices and took photographs of documents and other items the Soviets were determined to keep to themselves. So breaking into Dave's apartment was not a serious challenge. As he snored and reeked of used whiskey, the files and records on his smartphone and laptop were copied, his DNA was sampled, his apartment was mapped, and sophisticated listening and watching devices were planted so expertly that only a trained operator would find them. No one in his condo building was even aware the agents were in the building. Within fifteen minutes they were back in a nondescript white van heading east on Massachusetts Avenue.

***

Ossening enjoyed his morning coffee as he reviewed Dave's phone calls, text messages, emails and the stories he had filed. He knew where Dave went on the Internet and snickered at the images of naked Asian women at these sites, all offering private shows for a price. There was no record that Dave had ever paid for such services. He learned that Dave had an interest in antique firearms and Civil War relics. He learned that Dave and his girlfriend, Elena, had broken up. And he leaned that Dave had a serious drinking problem, which made him unstable and untrustworthy. This was the most troubling. Drunks were unreliable. They became belligerent and blamed everyone but themselves for their troubles. They said things and violated confidences and had no recollection. No, Dave Haggard was not a candidate for the loop.

But Ossening confirmed Dave's connection to Congressman Taylor and it made him smile as he congratulated himself on his instincts. The two men had talked on several occasions and Taylor had initiated meetings. That told Ossening that Taylor was working his own agenda. Dave was a passive passenger on Taylor's trip, wherever it was going.

He put the file in a locked drawer and opened a new one on Taylor. Ossening was on shaky ground. The F.B.I. had strict guidelines for investigating sitting members of Congress. He knew he was obligated to present his case to his superiors and receive approval to proceed, a process that might take months. He did not have months. He accessed a computer file on Taylor that offered the standard where-he-went-to-school background material and his military record. Taylor had made good grades all his life. He was nothing short of a Boy Scout. One item stood out. Taylor's military record did not reflect his intelligence training or assignments. Instead, the record showed that Taylor had spent two years at Ft. Eustis, Virginia with something called the Transportation Support Command. Such unit designations are often fronts for classified units that may not have ever been to their so-called home bases. Ossening knew that pursuing this with the Army would get him nowhere. It would also alert his superiors that he was investigating a sitting member of the House of Representatives and that would get him yet another crap assignment, this one far away from Washington, most likely in a remote field office where he would spend his career knocking on doors and asking questions of the friends of people who were applying for security clearances. Such assignments were as low as the F.B.I. got.

It convinced him that Taylor had friends in secret places. The task was to find those places and those friends.

Chapter Twenty-Five

Maskhadov liked his new look. He enjoyed the glances of women on Metro and it made him feel successful. He rode the trains from one end of the system to the other, initiating conversations when he could, presenting himself as a Russian businessman looking for opportunity in America. To each person who engaged him in conversation he offered "I love America!" several times, smiling. Most of the other passengers thought he was what he presented himself to be. A few thought he was kind of crazy. No one thought he was a terrorist.

He walked into downtown restaurants and studied other men in suits, noting their haircuts and fingernails. He studied the men's manners, how they held themselves when they spoke and when they ate.

He became confident that he could pass himself off as a businessman from Russia who loved America and wanted nothing more than to achieve the American Dream. Washington is a city of suits and it is easier to hide in plain sight if one looks and acts like everyone else.

Taylor's friends were searching for Maskhadov as he appeared when he escaped their surveillance, a bearded, threatening individual who looked out of place. They had no idea that he had changed his appearance, although the suggestion had come up at meetings and was dismissed. He was not considered smart enough to disguise himself.

Agents were stationed at the usual spots: Metro stations, the airports, Union Station, even the spots where cheap bus rides to New York were offered. There was no shortage of foreign-looking men with thick black beards, but Maskhadov was not among them. An agent was sent to the hookah bar in Frederick to see if he would return there. He did not. Agents went to Nationals Park to watch for him, assuming that, because it was his suspected target, he must show up at some point.

The agents were enraged by the photo of Ghazali, aka Gutierrez, shaking hands with a uniformed Secret Service agent outside the White House. The photo made them the laugh of the week within certain circles. Ghazali was another free agent on the loose. Supervisors pounded desks and agents pounded their sources, but neither target was seen.

***

Ghazali, for his part, was sleeping in Rock Creek Park at night and wandering urban neighborhoods during the day, checking the spots that had been designated as alternative drop sites when he was given his instructions about his mission. There was no sign of Maskhadov. Ghazali was patient. He ate in bars where Hispanic immigrants gathered to gossip and complain about their treatment in America. He asked if anyone had seen his "old friend" and described Maskhadov. No one had.

Maskhadov tired of his game of playing at being a Russian businessman and returned to his mission, confident that no one would know him. He knew that Ghazali was free and assumed the man was searching for him to kill him. It would be an easy matter to turn the tables on the stupid man. He knew what Ghazali looked like, Ghazali did not know what he looked like. Child's play.

He went to a small park on P Street Northwest and sat on a bench. He inserted a small piece of paper into a space between the vertical support and the seat, made a small mark with a piece of yellow chalk, and walked away. He found an outdoor café and took a table with a view of the bench. He sat for several hours, consuming coffee and rolls and engaging others in conversations about the greatness of America.

By dusk, he was growing tired of the game and stood to leave. It was then he noticed Ghazali staring at the bench and looking around the neighborhood for signs of Maskhadov. He sat on the bench and retrieved the paper, slipped it into his pocket, and walked away. The paper would instruct Ghazali to return in twenty-four hours. Maskhadov smiled. He looked up and down the street and tried to imagine the scene that would have the people who lived here running for their lives. Fools, he thought. Lambs.

***

An agent searching for both men was riding a bicycle along P Street, appearing to be a common hipster. The man was trained to look for body movement, eye contact, facial expression, and anything unusual about anyone. He rode past Maskhadov, nearly hitting him with the bike, as he headed toward the small park. He did not recognize him. The agent saw a man hurrying away from the park and jumped the curb to get closer. He recognized Ghazali and closed on him, riding by the man and snapping a photo with his phone. Ghazali was back in the trap. Maskhadov was walking in the opposite direction and missed the catch.

***

Higher ups in an underground Northern Virginia office decided that more agents were needed to keep an eye on Ghazali because he was clever and could slip his leash. Several of the agents complained about insect bites after one night in Rock Creek Park.

Ghazali slept under a green poncho in a heavily wooded area of the park that was within easy walking distance of city streets. He used a public restroom to freshen himself and he purchased new clothes at a small shop, changing in the store and emerging as a fresh-faced Hispanic man out to enjoy the morning. The agents following him were not fresh and they scratched their bites and brushed off the dirt and undergrowth as they tracked the man. They were relieved by a new team of agents shortly before nine. The new agents tracked Ghazali as he wandered the streets, eating fast food and stopping to rest on park benches.

In a case of oversight that would bring a round of recriminations, no one was assigned to watch the park where Ghazali had first been spotted, so they missed Maskhadov's appearance and the fake rock he planted near the bench where he had instructed Ghazali to be.

The hour came when Ghazali was to meet Maskhadov. He looked around and saw no one who appeared to be suspicious. He walked in several directions, backtracking on some streets, and approached the park. He was a block away when the explosion sent the park bench flying onto the roof of a nearby building. What appeared to be the body of a man cart wheeled over a tree and onto the awning of an outdoor restaurant. A cloud of smoke rose from the park as people on the street screamed and ran.

Ghazali thought the body on the awning must be Maskhadov. He also assumed that Maskhadov had killed himself while he was planting a bomb to kill Ghazali. He felt no compassion and praised Allah for taking his enemy. He left the area and spent the afternoon in the Museum of the American Indian on the Mall, appearing to be just another dark-skinned man admiring the work and culture of the First Americans.

***

Congressman Taylor's agent friends, O'Neil, Gant, Ossening, and D.C. police and platoons of investigators from federal agencies spent their afternoon trying to determine what had happened in the park and who was the man whose body was being left on the restaurant's awning as the crime scene technicians performed their work. The explosion was international news and the word "terrorist" was attached to every story filed by every one of the hundreds of reporters who crowded the police lines near the park.

The death toll was one, the man on the awning. A dozen or so bystanders were injured, mostly by flying bits of this and that. A few of the injuries were caused by pieces of the fake rock in which Maskhadov had hidden the bomb.

By sunset investigators had determined that the man on the awning was a city employee named William Dawkins who worked for the D.C. Department of Recreation. He was scouting the park for a city-sponsored art festival when he came upon what he recognized as a plastic rock. Out of curiosity, he picked it up and the explosives inside the rock went off as intended. Only it was not intended for Dawkins, a man who had a wife and three children waiting at home for him in a well-kept Northeast Washington rowhouse.

The man for whom the bomb was intended slept in a city homeless shelter that night and spent his evening chatting with other men who spoke Spanish, gossiping about the explosion in the park and speculating about who might have been responsible. Ghazali, again known as Gutierrez, was the only man in the city who knew who was responsible. He smiled and nodded at the speculation among the homeless men, grew weary of the talk, and fell asleep on a dirty mattress. His dreams were of revenge and martyrdom. Watching him sleep were five federal agents.

Chapter Twenty-Six

Dave Haggard was in a gaggle of reporters screaming at the D.C. Police Chief as she walked past a yellow tape that separated the news media from the scene of the bombing. He did not know her well enough to gain even a glance. She had a reputation as a leader who kept her distance from reporters and occasionally favored those whose reporting she felt properly expressed her own views of the department, which ran along the lines of her men and women being the best in the world. She waved and frowned and shook her head at the questions, not answering any of them. A department flack had already issued the standard "We're pursuing all avenues of investigation" boilerplate and the Feds were not even acknowledging the presence of the reporters, much less talking to them.

O'Neil, Gant and Ossening waved Dave away when he approached them. He tried several times to get them away from the crowd so he could get a feel for what was happening but they resisted. O'Neil growled "Get the fuck away from me" when Dave grabbed his elbow. Dave took it as a sign that whatever had happened, it was more than a bomb in a park.

Homeland Security arrived in force, sealing off the park from everyone, including the D.C. Police. The Chief was seen pointing her finger in the face of a Homeland higher-up and shouting at him while some of her officers cheered and applauded. Dave assumed that some serious ass-covering was already underway.

By midnight the bomb site was under a large tent and stadium-strength lights were brought in to illuminate the scene. William Dawkins' body was taken down from the restaurant awning and taken away in a D.C. Emergency Services ambulance while a crowd of city residents cried and shook their heads.

It was a humid, sweltering late summer night and federal agents sweated in the wind breakers that announced their agencies. F.B.I. D.E.A. HOMELAND SECURITY. A.T.F. O'Neil was wearing a POLICE windbreaker and wiping his face with a towel when Dave called to him shortly after one in the morning.

"Inspector, got a minute?" Dave's voice was low and friendly.

"Jesus, not now, Dave."

"Come on. What's happening? Nobody is saying anything. We barely got the ID on the dead guy. You must know something by now."

O'Neil lowered his head and looked around. "Coffee shop. One hour." He walked away from Dave and grabbed a bottle of water from an aid station that had been set up for the investigators. He did not turn and look at Dave.

***

By two in the morning Dave had found a back table at the coffee shop, away from the late night partiers who were trying to sober up enough to get home. He sipped a decaf and looked over his notes, which were sparse on facts and long on descriptions of the park and the buildings surrounding it. He had filed a steady flow of scene-setting reports about what was not known and had described the agents and officers who were going over all physical evidence and blah blah while he waited for something solid to report. He needed something stronger for the reports that would go out across the country during the morning rush hours that began in the East and moved West by time zone.

O'Neil walked in wearing a Nationals baseball cap and plain white shirt. He had left his POLICE windbreaker in his car and was hoping to be seen as just another late-nighter looking for coffee. He saw Dave and found a seat across the table.

"Fan hitting time in the valley," he said by way of opening.

"Meaning?"

"We've got some surveillance video showing the guy who planted the bomb and the guy who picked it up. We think we know the doer. The poor guy who got killed, this Dawkins, was just a nice guy doing his job."

"Who's the doer?"

"One of the guys who got away from the feds. We think he's the guy who is planning to blow up Nationals Park next week or thereabouts. The feds thought they had an eye on him but he got away. It seems he shaved off his beard and now looks like every other guy in the suit around here. Facial recognition picked it up, even without the beard."

"Damn! Good work." Dave was impressed.

"Oh, hold your praise. It seems he was trying to blow up the other guy who got away, the guy who was messing with the electric grid. He was spotted by an agent yesterday. Guess where? In the park that got blown up today. They have him under watch but nobody thought to watch the park where he was seen after he slipped away from the guys who like to think of themselves as the best in the world at tracking people. Big fuck up. Asses are in slings."

Dave stared at O'Neil for a full minute. "Do you know Congressman Taylor from the Intelligence Committee?"

"We know all about your friend, Dave. It was his boys who fucked up."

"I don't think they're his boys. They work for an agency he used to work with."

"Whatever. If Homeland decides to share all of this with the Intel Committee, your boy Taylor will be censured for not sharing what he knew with the others."

"So, what happened today?"

"Technically, it was yesterday. We see a guy, Maskhadov, as it turns out, coming into the park in a suit and carrying what appears to be a thick, legal-size briefcase. He sits at a bench and looks around. He gets up, goes behind the bench, takes the bomb disguised as a rock out of the briefcase and leaves it on the ground behind the bench. We assume this was shortly before he was to meet Ghazali or Gutierrez or whatever he's calling himself.

About ten minutes later the poor and late Mister Dawkins walks around the park, notices the fake rock, and goes to his final reward.

"What do you have about the other guy, Ghazali?" Dave was taking notes and kicking himself for not turning on the record feature on his phone.

"We have video from yesterday showing Ghazali at the same bench retrieving what appears to be a message in paper form that had been hidden under the slats of the bench. We also see Ghazali leaving the park and a man who turned out to be one of Taylor's agents trailing him. We know he spent the night in Rock Creek Park and spent today wandering around. He was about a block from the park when the bomb went off. He then played tourist all afternoon and is now sound asleep in a homeless shelter." O'Neil paused a took a sip of coffee. "Now you have it all. I want you to tell me everything you know about Taylor."

Dave explained how he had come to know Taylor and what the Congressman had told him. O'Neil listened without expression.

"We've got a shit storm here, Dave," O'Neil said. "This blast in the park was only a sample. Frankly, if these two guys can take off once, they can take off again. The problem is they are off the grid. They don't use phones or anything we can track. Ghazali's use of a laptop was something he needed to do to screw with the electric grid. He's smart. He won't do it again. Maskhadov is old school, probably trained by the KGB on its Cold War tactics. Everybody knows the N.S.A. is watching and listening. Hell, they're in every computer and phone in the world. Good news for us if the bad guys are online. Bad news if they dump that stuff and go back to paper and hand signals."

"What can I use?" Dave asked, holding up his notebook.

"First, most of this is deep background you got from quote someone close to the investigation. That will narrow it down to about a hundred people, meaning no one can trace to me. All of yesterday's secrets are out of the bag as Homeland goes on a tear about Taylor's guys' fuckup, so my guess is you will be sharing this scoop with half a dozen other reporters in the morning. Second, don't panic the populace with stuff about an imminent attack on Nationals Park or some other public site in D.C. It's just speculation, anyway."

"So I can use the part about the feds finding the two suspected terrorists who escaped surveillance and were responsible for the bomb in the park?"

"Hell, use the part about investigators looking into why the park was not under observation after one of the terrorists was seen leaving. Use the surveillance video stuff. It's damn near open season on this, Dave."

"Why are you telling me this?"

"We go way back, Dave. The more I see the more I think there ain't no good guys. Some are just badder than others. This thing could have been prevented. What's coming can also be prevented. But, like I said, if these two actors can slip the knot once, they can do it again and next time the boom will be a lot bigger."

Dave shook hands with O'Neil and caught a cab to Now News. The first feed to hundreds of radio stations went out at five o'clock. Dave filed six separate reports on what O'Neil had told him and a "special report" that ran for three and a half minutes as a stand-alone feed for stations wanting to carry it. He also filed a comprehensive report on all that he knew for the website, along with the audio reports. He recorded a video report in which he detailed what he knew.

He beat the competition by an hour and by the time the morning television newscasts were on the air, Dave owned the story and other reporters, even those who had their own sources, were left to be seen as followers. Once again, Now News telephones lines were jammed with callers who wanted to congratulate or condemn Dave Haggard.

Cable networks were unable to get through to invite him to be on their news and talks shows, so they sent limos along with the written invitation. Dave turned off his cell phone and stopped reading his email.

Sid called him into his office.

"Well, Ace, you've done it again. I don't know whether to laugh or cry. Go home. Get some sleep. We've got the followups. Call me when you wake up."

"What about the cable show. Do you want me to do them?"

"Up to you. Set some limits or they'll run you into the ground."

***

He appeared on three cable show, repeating everything he had put in his reports. He refused to answer any questions that called for him to speculate about anything.

By mid-afternoon he was dizzy with exhaustion. He went to his condo in hopes of being left alone. The Camaroonian at the desk was, as usual, cheerful and well-mannered.

"You have mail, Mr. Haggard." He held out two envelopes.

Dave took them to his apartment and flopped onto his bed. He leaned back and opened the first letter. It was from Elena. "Fuck you!" was all it said.

The second had no return address nor any other identifier. It was a one line message.

This is the second time we tell you it is possible to know too much.

Chapter Twenty-Seven

The man who called himself Gutierrez went to Dupont Circle posing as a day laborer looking for work. He sat on a park bench with other such men and quietly waited to be approached by someone looking for cheap labor. The men were quiet because D.C. police patrolled the park and rousted the day laborers and ordered them to leave or face fines, which none of them could pay. The city had labor laws and the bureaucracy had no patience for anyone who had not filled out the proper forms.

The day was hot and the talk was about the explosion the previous day. The men whispered their speculation and passed along any rumor that seemed plausible to them, which included almost anything short of men from outer space.

He sat and watched the young professionals walk by with their expensive coffee and veggie wraps, wearing the uniform of the city, suits or khakis. What would they look like dead? he wondered. His hatred was hidden behind his smile. He watched the time pass on a digital clock outside a bank branch on Massachusetts Avenue. At two in the afternoon he left the circle and walked north to the Duke Ellington Bridge on Calvert Street. The bridge spanned

Rock Creek and Beach Drive through the city's largest park. He had read somewhere that it was a favorite spot for suicides. He idly wondered whether he would see such an event.

He found a spot that took him down into the park and a path that led to his destination, an alternative drop spot. He checked to make sure his handgun was tucked into the waistband of his pants. He wore a loose guayabera shirt that covered his belt line and the gun. The drop point was one on a list of alternatives in the event that one or more of the others became unavailable. The first site near the Islamic Center had been used and was no longer on the list. The park bench on P Steet was destroyed. Now number three was in play. He expected to find evidence that Maskhadov was or had been there, given the Chechen's attempt to kill him.

Ghazali smiled as he left the path and made his way through a patch of wild roses that slowed his movement as he picked off the thorns that tore at his clothing. He moved behind a large oak tree and sat down, peering down at the meeting spot. He looked up to see if he was being followed and saw nothing. The tree offered shade from the day's heat and he relaxed, wishing he had brought water.

***

It was two hours before Maskhadov appeared. The man was wearing a suit and tie, something that caused Ghazali to laugh out loud. The sound did not carry to Maskhadov, who scanned the area with small binoculars. The spot was a clearing about a hundred feet from the parkway that ran through the park. There were signs that picnickers had been there. A used condom was hanging from a bush at the edge of the clearing and a wine bottle with wilted wildflowers was propped up against a tree.

Maskhadov removed an envelope from his coat pocket. He left it under the wine bottle and walked down to the parkway and disappeared. Ghazali was too far away for an accurate shot so he watched the man and vowed that he would soon be dead. He waited fifteen minutes and went to the clearing to retrieve the envelope. He folded it, slid it into a pocket, and walked back to Dupont Circle, where he opened it and read its message.

Let us make peace. Tomorrow here. Same time.

Ghazali assumed that it was a ruse, an attempt to get him to let down his guard and believe that Maskhadov was genuine in his desire to end the war between them. His honor told him that an attempt on his life gave no quarter to Maskhadov. The man had to die. He tore the paper to small pieces and dropped it into a trash can.

He left the park and walked east down Massachusetts Avenue toward 14th Street, which would take him to the shelter for the night. He planned to make one stop on the way to the shelter. He would deliver a message to a man who was becoming a problem. The man's name and address had been given to him by Maskhadov at a drop a week earlier. Maskhadov referred to him as the man who knows too much. As he neared 17th Street he saw the man staring him. The man's face lit up with recognition. He walked over and offered his hand.

"Hello. I'm Dave Haggard. I'm the reporter who interviewed you after that explosion in Cambridge, Maryland. Do you remember me?"

Ghazali backed up and his right hand moved behind him to the gun. "No. I don't know you. I'm not from here." He tried to sound like a Hispanic man struggling with English.

"I know. You live in Cambridge. A house blew up. I talked with you. You saw it. Remember?" Dave was positive it was the same man. Years as a street reporter had given him a memory for faces. What he saw now as a man who appeared to be trying to escape a trap.

"No, no. I don't know you. Don't talk to me." Ghazali kept his hand behind his back as he moved past Dave and at 17th Street he broke into a run. Dave was outside his apartment building and was on his way to get something to eat when the man appeared.

He called O'Neil. "I think I can disprove your idea that there's no such thing as a coincidence," he said by way of opening the conversation.

"How's that?"

"I just ran into a guy who was the house explosion in Cambridge where that software guy was killed. I talked to him there but he denies he ever saw me before and he ran, literally ran away. I'm sure it was him."

"What'd he look like?"

"Hispanic, thirtyish, fit."

"Could be possibly be Pakistani?"

"Well, yeah, I suppose so."

"Get a photo?"

"Nope."

"Coffee shop. Fifteen minutes."

O'Neil was there when Dave arrived, staring at his phone. "You ever play games on your phone?" he asked, when Dave sat down.

"I try not to."

"These things are amazing." He looked at Dave with his Officer Friendly face. "I have something for you to look at." He slid a photo across the table. It was the image of Ghazali shaking hands with a Uniformed Secret Service Officer outside the White House. "This the guy?"

Dave looked at the photo. There was no doubt. "That's him."

O'Neil shook his head. "Bad actor. Now we know who killed Rodell Clark, the guy who wrote the software that was supposed to protect the electric grid. He sold out and it looks like he fell in with a bad crowd. Which way did this guy go?"

"East down Massachusetts from 17th. On foot."

Neither man was made privy to the fact that federal agents knew exactly where Ghazali was. The walls between agencies had gone up again, barely twenty-four hours after the explosion in the small park off P Street.

O'Neil stood and offered his hand. "I'll put this into the system. Watch your back."

"By the way," Dave said. "I got another note about me knowing too much."

"Watch your back," O'Neil said, hurrying out the door.

Chapter Twenty-Eight

Agent Patricia Gant was summoned to the Hoover Building to discuss her current assignment and her relationship with O'Neil. Of particular concern to her superiors was the absence of a request to return to the F.B.I.'s field service. Even agents who were understood to be on backwater assignments as punishment for one sin or another were expected to file requests to be removed from such assignments and be welcomed back into the fold. Agent Gant had accepted her assignment to the Capital Area Task Force On Security, CATFOS, a depository for agents, cops, analysts and others who had run afoul of their various agencies policies, cultures, or ego-inflated bosses

Gant was headstrong and smart. The F.B.I. likes smart. It does not like headstrong, especially in cases where a lower-ranking agent makes no secret of her contempt for her superiors' capacity to understand even basic law enforcement. Gant had been a star-quality lawyer before joining the Bureau and saw herself as at least one layer above the riff raff at the Hoover Building and its outposts.

Given all this, her superiors were dismayed when they failed to receive a stream of heated requests to be assigned to something more prestigious and action-oriented than CATFOS, a collection of losers, in the minds of those who sent her there.

***

Gant was wearing a designer suit and expensive pumps as she entered the building. The suit was well-tailored and displayed the figure of a woman who knew how to take care of herself. Her chocolate skin was flaw-less. Her hair was cut and fashioned. She looked straight ahead as agents and security guards gaped. She was wear-ing a thin smile. They had made the first move and she knew she would get any assignment she wanted.

She went to a fourth floor conference room and sat alone for thirty-minutes. She knew those who had called the meeting were asserting their power over her time. She didn't care. Two men and a woman entered the room wearing the standard-issue F.B.I. face, friendly but not inviting any closeness.

One of the men was Bud Ossening, himself a shit-listee but for different reasons. Ossening was carrying a file which Gant assumed was hers. The other man was introduced and Gant immediately dismissed him as some-one assigned to the meeting as a witness to whatever was going to transpire. The woman was identified as Agent Moore. She did not offer her hand nor did she speak.

Ossening opened the file. "So, you and Inspector O'Neil appear to have a good working relationship. Is that correct?"

"Yes," Gant replied.

"Good. I also have a long history with the Inspector and I find him to be a competent, if occasionally unorthodox, law enforcement officer." Ossening glanced at the agents who had accompanied him to the meeting and nodded. They nodded back.

"May I ask why I have been called to this meeting?" Gant said, glancing at the others.

"This won't take long," Ossening said. "It has come to our attention that the two of you are working on an investigation into two men who may be suspects in yesterday's bombing at the park on P Street. Is that correct?"

"We have been following a few leads relating to the death of a man whom we interviewed about the power outages. The man's name was Rodell Clark. He escaped during our questioning and was later murdered."

"And you have been observed talking with a reporter named Dave Haggard. Is that correct?"

"We have had conversations with him, yes, but we have not shared any confidential information with him or any other journalist." Gant sat back and allowed Ossening to explain why she was here.

"Would it surprise you to know that Haggard is also getting information from a member of Congress who is on the Intelligence Committee of the House?"

"No, it would not. I assume that journalists work every source they can."

"True. Well, we know you are unhappy where you are. You have not filed requests for reassignment but you're feelings are well known. We have a new assignment for you. Would you like to know what it is?"

"First, let me be clear and state that I have never shared with anyone my feelings about my current assignment, good or bad. Second, I'm sure I will informed of my new duties when it is deemed proper to do so." She glared at Ossening.

"Due time is here. You are to form a task force to find and neutralize the two and maybe more men who are planning a terrorist attack. A number of agents and officers are chasing these guys all over the area and no one has a handle on it. Here's the file. Agent Moore here will work with you. You can put O'Neil on the team if you like. You have twenty-four hours to get the team in place. There are some spooks over in Virginia following two men and you're probably already aware that these guys are better than the spooks who are trying to keep an eye on them. We need to know what and where and we need to know right now. Good luck, Agent Gant." With that, Ossening pushed the file over to Gant and left the room with the other man.

***

Gant and Moore looked at each other as Gant opened the file. Inside was everything she already knew and much more. "You have field experience?"

"I'm an analyst," Moore said.

"Analyze this," Gant said, pointing to the file.

"They want to blow up Nationals Park. They know how to do it. It's our job to stop them. That's about it."

Gant chuckled. "Right on. Do we have an office or a desk?"

"This is it."

"Get what you need. I have to make some calls." An hour later O'Neil was reassigned to Gant's team, along with seven F.B.I. agents Gant admired. By eight that night she was holding her first meeting and by midnight federal agents who thought they were working for Congressman Taylor's friends found themselves working for Gant.

She picked up a legal pad and scratched letters on the pages. She taped the pages to the wall of the conference room. It read *NO MORE BULLSHIT!*

Chapter Twenty-Nine

Dave Haggard's phone had been busy for twelve hours. Word was leaking out all over Washington that the F.B.I. had pulled rank on other agencies and had very high level orders to form a special task force using whatever resources it needed. It was also ordered that all agencies share whatever information and intelligence they had regarding what was now a level one threat. The task force was headed by Agent Patricia Gant, who, in an instant, had become the most powerful anti-terrorist cop in the city.

Dave was surprised at how many people knew he had been meeting with Gant and O'Neil. Reporters from other news organizations had heard rumors and called to see if it was true. Justice Department flacks called to fish for information he might be willing to share. Congressman Taylor called to arrange a meeting. O'Neil called to say they needed a more secure place for their coffee meets.

***

Dave met Taylor at a small café near Nationals Park. The team was out of town and the place was nearly empty. He wore a Tennessee Volunteers cap and glasses with thick, black frames. It took Dave a minute to recognize him.

"Nice disguise," Dave said, pulling up a chair.

"I need these to read," Taylor said, pointing at his glasses.

"Are you doing a lot of reading?"

"It's a busy time. What do you know about this Gant woman?"

"Not much. I've met her a couple of times. She doesn't say much and hates reporters."

"So do I but that doesn't stop me from talking to you." Taylor had a smile on his face but his voice was cold.

"What can I do for you, Congressman?"

"You know the problem with intelligence work? The problem is the word intelligence. Sometimes there's not much of it in the strictest sense. You know what I mean?"

"Not really."

"We gather information but we don't know what to do with it. Sometimes we sit on it and other times we pass it around like playing cards. That's what happened here. The team I'm kind of playing for did a great job to a point but then it fell apart. In short, we screwed this up." Taylor looked at Dave and waited for a response.

"And...?" Dave raised his eyebrows.

"And now we have what we Army types used to call a clusterfuck. The real question is whether we are more or less organized than the men we are watching, assuming they haven't slipped the knot again."

"Why don't you just pick them up? You know they're up to no good and will probably blow something up if they get a chance. Why give them the chance?"

"You're thinking like a civilian. We don't know who these guys know. We need to find out who they answer to. They are the part of the iceberg that's sticking up. We want to find out what's below the water line."

"Are they part of some kind of network?"

"Duh. These guys didn't just wash up on America's shores with a fully formed plan. They answer to people who answer to people and so on up the pipe."

"How far are you willing to let this go?"

"That's not for me to answer. It's now up to Agent Gant and her brand new task force. Maybe you two can have a cup of coffee and talk it over."

"Like I said, she's hates reporters."

"Maybe your friend Inspector O'Neil can help you there." Taylor drained his cup and stood up. "Let's do this again some time."

***

Dave called O'Neil and set up a meeting at Roosevelt Island in the Potomac. The island is a wild spot in the river between Georgetown and Roslyn, a trendy area of Arlington. The island is an eighty-eight acre park managed by the National Park Service. It's a memorial tribute to Theodore Roosevelt, an enthusiastic outdoorsman. The park is heavily wooded and its trails offer secluded spots for reflection and, given its location, clandestine meetings of all kinds.

The island was within walking distance of Now News and the heavy summer air had Dave sweating by the time he crossed the bridge to the island and found comfort in the shade of the large trees that welcomed visitors. O'Neil was waiting by a statue of Roosevelt, reading the inscription.

Dave tapped him on the shoulder. "Aren't you supposed to be hard to sneak up on?"

"It's a myth. Let's take a walk." The two men walked to a swampy area where the path was a wooden walkway. The humidity from the water and the mosquitos combined to make it unpleasant enough to drive away everyone else.

"So, you have a new boss," Dave said

"I don't have a boss, Dave. This was something Ossening pulled off at the Hoover Building. He may not be a rising star but he knows how the game is played. As I told you before, things were falling apart and needed to be organized. Gant's the person to do it. She can kick ass. Ossening convinced some of the Bureau's brass that the F.B.I. had what it takes to get a handle on it and the White House bought it."

"What's next?"

"Right now, hurt feelings. Taylor's friends are screaming that their toes are being stepped on. Homeland Security's claiming they have jurisdiction so they want to meeting this thing to death. In other words, same old Washington game."

"And how about the terrorists, Ghazali and Maskhadov? Are they still on the chain?"

"At the moment. We're gonna put some pressure on them to flush out their friends, if they have any, and to get them to make mistakes. We think Ghazali will try to hit Maskhadov but we don't know if it will be before or after whatever they have in mind. We've got eyes on Nationals Park. We've got eyes on these two jokers. We're going to advance the ball, so to speak."

"When?"

"Stay by your phone."

"Anything I can report?" Dave waved his phone.

"If that thing is on I'll stomp it and toss it into the river. No, nothing now."

***

An hour later Dave and Sid were staring at each other and reviewing their options, which were few at the moment. Dave not could use what he knew. Now News had already claimed the story. News is like good French bread. Good when it's fresh and stale tomorrow.

Sid sat back and gazed at the ceiling. "So, it seems, we wait."

Chapter Thirty

Maskhadov parked on Beach Drive and walked a hundred yards to the meeting spot. His rental car was left under a tree to shade it. The road crossed Rock Creek and he stopped to enjoy the water and delighted in the small fish that were visible in the sunlight. His attention was on the moment and he failed to see the shadow that moved to the far side of his car and attach a GPS device. Those who were tracking him had intended that the shadow be noticed by the target. It was not.

He resumed his walk and smiled as he strolled to the meeting site with the air of a man out for a lovely stroll on a summer day. A casual observer would believe that the man in the suit found himself with a moment to spare and chose to spend it in the wonders of nature.

Ghazali was again behind the oak tree, handgun drawn, and waiting. He had no desire to make peace. He wanted Maskhadov to be within twenty-five yards before he fired. Handguns were not the most accurate weapons at distance and he planned to fire two quick rounds and make his escape. He tried to control his breathing and inhaled and exhaled slowly, but his heart was beating fast and he became short of breath, which caused him breathe faster. He sounded like a buck snorting in the forest by the time Maskhadov was within range.

"I know you are there," Maskhadov shouted. "I can't see you but I hear you. Do not shoot me. It would not be good for you."

Ghazali was startled and tried to control his breaths, which got faster and louder. "You must die. Death to you!"

"Oh, my friend. We have much to discuss. Come out so we can talk."

"No talking. Come closer so I can shoot you." Ghazali's voice had a hysterical quality.

"Come out. Don't you see we must work together."

Ghazali's mind was racing. He could not concentrate. He felt faint. "You are an evil man," he shouted.

"No more evil than you, my friend. Nowhere near as evil as those we seek to destroy."

"How can I trust you?"

"Look behind you. There are men watching us. Do you want to end up in one of their prisons and live like an animal. Come, let us get out of here."

Ghazali looked behind him and saw two men in suits watching them from the bridge. He gauged whether they could catch him if he ran and he decided he had at least a two minute advantage. He sprang from behind the tree and ran in Maskhadov's direction and two of them raced to the rental car under the tree. The men who had been watching the car retreated to allow the two fugitives to climb inside and drive away.

One of the men lifted his wrist to his mouth and radioed the others. "Game on," he said.

Agent Gant responded, "You had to do everything but wave a flag to let them know you were there. Don't lose them."

"Roger that."

***

Maskhadov and Ghazali drove onto Connecticut Avenue due north into Maryland and took the Beltway to Prince Georges County and out Route 50 to the Bay Bridge over to Kent Island on the Eastern Shore. Neither man spoke until Maskhadov pulled into a tourist motel and parked.

"We are again the hunted," he said. "Stay here. I will get a room where we can talk."

Ghazali was dizzy. He was still debating whether to work with Maskhadov or kill him. He remained silent as the Chechen got out and walked into the small office where a pimply-faced teenage boy was behind the desk. The boy was wearing a "Shit Happens" t-shirt and pretended to be busy as Maskhadov waited to be noticed.

When the boy looked up and casually asked, "May I help you?" Maskhadov smiled and presented himself as a friendly man looking for a place to rest.

"I and my companion need a room that is quiet and away from the traffic. Do you have rooms in back?"

The boy smirked. "Companion. Ain't that what homos say when they talk about their boyfriends?"

"We are not homosexuals. We are friends, nothing more, and we need a room. Do you have something in the back?"

"Yep. We got em. Hunnert fitty a night."

"What's that?"

"Hunnert fitty. You're probly foreign. I'll write it out." The boy wrote 150 on a piece of scrap paper and pushed it across the country.

"Yes, yes. We'll take it," Maskhadov said.

"How many nights?"

"I don't know. I will pay in cash for tonight."

Again, the boy smirked. "I get it. You don't want nobody to know so you ain't payin' with a credit card. We get that all the time. Make it two hunnert and I won't even write down your license plate."

Maskhadov debated whether to give the boy another fifty dollars and decided it would make no difference. The boy could not be trusted. He would deal with him later if he had time. "No, the one-fifty will be fine. I have nothing to hide."

Maskhadov and Ghazali settled into a small, musty room that was shielded from Route 50 and stared at each other.

"What do we do?" Ghazali asked.

"We move ahead with the plan. They will find us again. We must move fast. Let us make peace with each other."

"I suppose we have no choice," Ghazali said.

"We must put the plan in motion. I will rent a truck and we can load our supplies in it and make ready."

"I must rest," Ghazali said. He lay back on the bed and closed his eyes.

***

Maskhadov left the room and drove to a truck rental lot in the small town of Stevensville, where he used a fake driver's license to rent a small moving van. He drove it to a strip mall a mile away, returned to retrieve the rental car, and drove it to a lot near the Bay and set it on fire, first removing the plates, which he dumped into the Bay.

Agent Gant's team watched from a distance and took notes. One of them idly wondered if the GPS tracking device would have to be accounted for and who would pay for it. No one worried about the rental car.

Chapter Thirty-One

Ghazali awoke to find Maskhanov gone along with the rental car. It was dark. He assumed that he had been abandoned or that Maskhanov would come back to kill him. He cursed himself for believing that a peace between them had been achieved. He was reassured of his safety when he felt the gun still in his belt line. It was loaded. He would not go to his reward without a fight.

He left the room to walk the perimeter and watched as cars sped by on Route 50 on their way to Ocean City or Rehobeth Beach. Families of dads, moms and kids smiling and anticipating their days at the beach. Such happiness was denied to Ghazali's people and he hated those who drove past him. *Soon, you will know.*

His thoughts drifted to his mission and his betrayal. He had merely been a pawn in Maskhadov's game, nothing more than a diversion. He walked to a bench near the motel's office and sat to take the air and plan his next move. Something caught his eye. A man in a car parked in a dark area away from the road. Ghazali had been trained to use his night vision and knew that objects in the dark were difficult to see if one looked directly at them, so he looked away a few degrees and saw a silhouette. At first glance it appeared to be nothing more than the headrest on the driver's side but it moved. A hand. Whoever was sitting in the car was tired and wiped his hand over his face, perhaps to rub his eyes.

Ghazali knew that the man in the car was watching him. It was surely not Maskhadov. He would not be hiding. The hair on his neck stood up as he realized that he and Maskhadov had not escaped their surveillance. They had merely been allowed to think they had shaken their observers.

Where was Maskhadov? Had they taken him? If so, why was he, Ghazali, still at the motel sitting on a bench in plain sight? They were being played. Those who had sent him to find Maskhanov were still there, watching.

As he pondered his predicament he saw a rental moving van pull into the parking lot and go around to the back. He glanced at the car where his observer was watching and casually walked to the truck, where Maskhanov was backing in to the space in front of their room.

"We are being watched," Ghazali said.

"How do you know?" Maskhanov's face was angry.

"There's a man in a car in front. There may be others. We did not get away from them."

"You're sure?"

"We are well trained, are we not?"

"Let me look around. Go inside and get our things." Maskhanov walked to the edge of the parking lot and found a grassy area that led to the rear of a small strip mall.

Ghazali was back within a minute and the two men climbed into the truck. Maskhanov kept the lights off as he drove over the grass to the paved area behind the small mall and around to the front where the stores were closing. He continued onto a two lane road that led away from Route 50 toward the bay. He risked keeping the lights off until they were well away from anyone who might be looking for movement from them.

He drove all night over back roads that led into Delaware and when dawn broke the two men were assaulted by the smells coming from the area's chicken farms. There was no one following them. They had managed to escape again, but they knew their time was short.

***

Patricia Gant was furious. Her team was assembled at six in the morning at a hotel meeting room on Kent Island and the faces looking back at her were red with embarrassment.

"Do you want to know how the bad guys win?" She glared at each of them. "They win when bozos like you let them win. You all are supposed to be the experts in this. Well-trained, motivated, smart. You are the keepers of the public's safety. What do I do now? Call for the evacuation of Washington because so-called professionals can't keep an eye on two guys? What were you thinking?"

She turned to an agent named Harrison. "You were keeping an eye on the motel and these guys just drove off. Were you sleeping? Jerking off? Reading your email? Give me an answer."

Harrison shrank back into his chair. "I have no excuse."

"No, you don't. Nor do the rest of you. Whose idea was it to leave Harrison alone to watch these guys?"

An Army security agent named Boston raised his hand. "Mine."

"Explain."

"No excuse."

"Was there no one else available?"

"No excuse." Boston looked like a schoolboy caught reading a naughty book.

"Damn right there's no excuse." Gant slapped her hand on the table. "Here's what going to happen. You all are going to find these guys and you will have no time off, no rest, no sleep, nothing until we have eyeballs on Maskhadov and Ghazali. Understood?"

There were mutterings around the table from the men and women who were exhausted from lack of sleep and who faced an unknown number of hours or days until they could rest.

"Let's begin with the truck. Find it."

Thirty-Two

Maskhadov and Ghazali drove into the town of Milford, Delaware as the store owners were opening for the day. The town is used to the sight of beachgoers passing through on their way to the shore or Cape Henlopen State Park, so the truck drew no attention. A few people on the sidewalks glanced at it but no one would remember the truck or its occupants. The truck proceeded north on Route 1 into a rural area where Maskhadov turned right onto a blacktop road that led to Delaware Bay. He found a gravel road that disappeared into a stand of trees and turned onto it, driving slowly. He saw no one.

He drove into the treed area and saw that wild roses had invaded the ground beneath the oaks and pines and he pulled the truck in as far it would go before it became tangled in the underbrush and stopped. The two men got out, pulling thorns from their clothing, and gathered tree branches, pine boughs, and any other vegetation that could be picked up to cover the truck. A man walking along the gravel road might not notice it at a casual glance. A man within ten or twenty feet would surely see that a truck was under the greenery but that was a chance they would have to take.

They walked along the blacktop without speaking. Ghazali assumed they were walking west toward Milford but the sky was cloudy and he could not find the sun. Maskhadov was gloomy.

The men rounded a bend and saw a police car heading toward them about a half mile away. They kept walking and waved to the officer, a chubby young man who waved back. They turned off the road and crossed a field to a copse of pine trees where they hid from the road and waited for the police officer to return. An hour passed and the cop car did not appear, so they resumed their walking, this time away from the road.

A muddy work pickup truck was parked in a field where a large hole had been dug. The truck had a magnetic sign on its door that read Utility Contractor. Thick cables were snaking out of the hole. The men stopped. Maskhadov measured their chances of stealing the truck. If men were in the hole they might get away. If the men were nearby and saw Maskhadov and Ghazali there would be a fight that they would lose. Maskhadov assumed that men who worked in holes in the ground were strong and could fight.

There was no movement at the hole. The cables did not move. There was no sound. "Go see who is there," Maskhadov ordered.

"Why me? You go." Ghazali said.

"Don't' be a shaz," Maskhadov said, using an Arabic word for deviant.

"Do not call me that," Ghazali said, raising a fist.

"Calm down. It was a joke. Wait here." Maskadov walked up to the site with a smile on his face, prepared to ask directions to Milford and ask if the workmen knew where he could find a job. There was no one in the hole and no sign of the men who had been working in it. He saw that a second truck has been there, its tires had spun in the moist earth that still emitted the scent of recently turned soil. The workmen were gone, Maskhadov assumed it was a quick trip to pick up a needed part or perhaps food.

He checked the pickup and saw that the keys were in the ignition. He climbed in, started the vehicle, and drove to Ghazali, who did not wait for an explanation before he jumped in.

***

The chubby police officer who had waved at Maskhodov and Ghazali was first to respond to the call that a truck missing from a work site. The two men who were doing the utility work were pacing the ground when he arrived. The young officer was a local boy named Arland Spanak. He had grown up with the nickname of Spanks. The two workmen who waited for him to park the patrol car had known him all his life.

"Goddam it, Spanks. What took you so long?" the older of the two said.

"Hold your horses, Ed. What's going on?"

"Somebody stole my damn truck, that's what's going on."

Officer Spanak looked from one man to the other. "You leave your keys in it?"

"What's that got to do with anything? Hell, if a man can't leave his truck out in a damned field, what's the use of living in the country? You need to get on your radio and put out an all points bulletin." The man's face was red and he leaned into Spanak.

"Well, first let's review what happened." The officer pulled out a notebook and a pencil. "Did either of you see anything suspicious or anyone who looked like he might be thinking of stealing your truck?"

It was thirty minutes before Office Spanak put out an all points bulletin for the truck. It would be two hours before he remembered the two men who waved to him on the road.

It would be six hours before Gant's team arrived at the scene and by then the pickup truck and its occupants were in Frederick, Maryland, where they abandoned the pickup and stole a large cargo van.

The van was loaded with the supplies the men had gathered and was on its way to Washington.

The stolen pickup was discovered the next morning by young man who was sneaking a joint behind a warehouse at the edge of the town. He finished his joint and told his supervisor that a pickup with Delaware plates had been left on the property. The supervisor waited until the end of his shift to pass the word along to the warehouse manager, who called police.

It was midnight before Gant's team was informed that the truck was in Frederick. Everyone on the team knew that it meant nothing other than another pin on a map. The men they were pursuing could be anywhere by now. Gant knew that both Markhodov and Ghazali had one destination. She sent a team to Nationals Park.

Chapter Thirty-Three

Dave Haggard had been dry for two days. He assumed that a couple of days with no booze would clear his head and make him feel better. It did not. He felt terrible. His mind was clogged by something that felt like fog or cotton. He stomach hurt. His eyes were yellow and lined with red. His tongue had a sickly slickness that felt like slime in his mouth. He decided to give it one more day. If he didn't feel better he would have a couple of drinks to see what that did for him.

He was idly staring at a computer screen in the newsroom, wondering where to go with a story about a Justice Department program to educate elderly consumers about cyber theft. He had no feeling for it. Everyone knew about cyber theft so what else was there to say? He was having angry thoughts about old people who needed a Justice Department press release to help them out. He banged out a boiler-plate one minute piece and went into a studio to record it. The guy working the desk messaged him that Sid wanted a ninety-second piece for the evening feed, so he wrote and recorded it, using much of the same language he had pasted into the first piece. It was days like this that made him wonder if he had been a street reporter for too long. Chasing a big story was one thing. Pumping life into a press release was something else.

His phone rang with its dobro ringtone. He looked at it and saw that Ossening was calling from the F.B.I. Maybe the day could be salvaged. "Hello. Dave Haggard here."

"Can you get to the Navy Memorial in fifteen minutes?" Ossening wasted no words with greetings or salutations.

"On my way."

Ossening was sitting on steps watching a young woman in a light summer dress. He smiled as Dave sat next to him. "See her? That is why I believe in God. In a world of hurt and bullshit along comes a vision in a summer dress and all is right for a few seconds. It's God's way of saying he's sorry for all the trouble."

Dave glanced at the woman, whose dark hair hung over her shoulders. She had soft eyes and a thin body. She reminded him of Elena, who was now fighting to be erased from his memory. "She's nice."

"Do you think she's a tourist or just a local girl who goes around making people happy to see her?" Ossening was in a strange mood.

"She's alone, so she's probably not a tourist. Maybe she works around here." Dave wondered where this was going.

"Did you know that we are being videoed as we sit here? There are cameras all over this part of the city. There's facial recognition software that will pick up certain people who are on watch lists. Criminals, terrorists, high ranking government officials, journalists who cover those officials, journalists who are on the national security beat. Both of us qualify. Hell, we might be on some big screen right now. Were you aware of that?"

"Sort of. You hear things in this city. I've read about the cameras. I didn't know about the watch lists."

"I just want you to know this is not a clandestine meeting."

"About?"

"Our friends have slipped the knot again and all hell is breaking loose around us. Did O'Neil tell you about the task force that Agent Gant is heading? She's been handed the shit job of either finding and stopping these guys or taking the fall if it all goes south. So far, it's been a cluster fuck. The so-called expert special operators who are working for your Congressman Taylor's friends have not proved themselves to be as good as advertised and now things are what the military types call maximum pucker factor."

"What does that mean?"

"It means that the ball is in the bad guys' court and the next move is theirs. Gant has Nationals Park under surveillance but that might not do the trick, given how these guys are outsmarting us. The play seems to be there. Right now the debate at the Hoover Building is whether to call off the series with the Dodgers and panic the populace or try to get ahead of this."

"Who's winning?"

"Hell if I know." Ossening had the look of a man who was about to leave for the beach.

"Why are you telling me this?"

"Just a heads up. Whatever happens it will be soon."

Dave needed a drink and eyed a trendy bar a block away. It was the kind of place that drew millennials who liked candy-tasting drinks that cost more than a six pack of beer. He had no desire for a drink that would be a hit at an elementary school. He wanted something that said hard liquor. He also wanted a cigarette, which he had given up a year earlier. He spent a moment in self-pity, asking himself why it was wrong for a man to enjoy himself with his vices. A smoke and a drink. He recalled the story of a United States Senator from Texas who would travel around the state campaigning and at each town he would pull aside a local official and demand a fifth of whiskey and a woman. The man served four terms, so it must have been okay, at least back then.

It was the middle of the day and he had to get back to New News and brief Sid about his talk with Ossening. Sid would throw him out if he smelled alcohol. He hailed a cab and brooded about his life. Sid told him to join a gym and clean himself up. He found a note from Elena in his mailbox. *I'm going back to New York. Don't follow me. You're an asshole.* Damn. The last time she had left for New York he had stayed in Washington and let her go. When she came back she shouted at him for not chasing her. He assumed this was another of her *come after me* notes. He had no energy for this. He tossed the note into a trash can and sat at a work station to read the wires and catch up on what was happening around the world. His head hurt and his stomach demanded food. Or a drink.

Chapter Thirty-Four

O'Neil let Gant vent. She was pounding her desk with an open hand, convinced that there was not one competent agent or officer on her team. No one had seen anything. "I could get some Boy Scouts in here and they would do a better job," she shouted. "I can see the headlines now. 'Keystone Cops miss chance to prevent catastrophe. All is lost.' Do you think the bad guys know how incompetent we are?"

O'Neil sat and listened without responding. He had years of experience with rants, his own and others, and knew that, like tornadoes, they burned themselves out. He also knew that Gant's next phase would be action. She would get up from her desk and storm out. It took an hour. He followed her into the elevator and down to the garage where she climbed into an F.B.I. car and pointed to the passenger side. "Get in," she said.

She parked the car two blocks from Nationals Park. "Let's see what the boys are up to," she said. She and O'Neil walked the perimeter she had established as a surveillance area where her agents were to watch for Maskhadov and Ghazali. Cameras had been positioned on nearby buildings and in the construction sites where new buildings were replacing the seedy establishments that had given the neighborhood a down-in-the-heels feel before the stadium was built. The area had the feel of a giant development, which it was. Washington professionals, construction workers, leftovers from sadder days, hustlers selling caps and bottled water all mingled on the sidewalks in the shadow of the ballpark.

Two of her agents were dressed as construction workers. Two others were working as waiters in an outdoor restaurant. Others were in cars. She had no trouble spotting them, although she doubted anyone else could pick them out of a crowd. A van parked in a construction zone monitored the cameras.

She used a small radio to contact the van. "Do we have anyone in the stadium?"

"Not today. There's no game." The responding agent had the tone of a woman who was tired.

"I want someone in the stadium at all times," Gant said.

"Who do we pull off the street?" The tired voice had no energy.

"Pick someone," Gant said.

She and O'Neil went to the centerfield gate and displayed their credentials to the bored rent-a-cop who was leaning against a post, reading a magazine. The guard waved them in and went back to the magazine.

The stadium was quiet. A few groundskeepers were grooming the infield. The outfield grass was brilliant green and had been criss-cross cut to give it a plaid appearance. It was a state-of-the-art ballpark and it drew tens of thousands of fans to almost every game. Gant looked around and it appeared to her that the park was nearly indestructible. How could anyone blow it up? She was no expert on explosives and knew next to nothing about structural engineering, but to her only a fool would think it could be brought down with a homemade bomb.

Still, she thought, a bomb in a crowd could do a lot of damage. She shuddered as she remembered the bombing at the Boston Marathon. The memory made her angry and she vowed to take down Maskhodov and Ghazali before they could hurt anyone. She briefly considered requesting permission to shoot both men on sight, but thought better of it. Permission would never be granted, not in an age when media and Congressional snoops had access to everything everywhere. The age of privacy was over for everyone, the F.B.I. included, she thought.

O'Neil recognized a detective from the D.C. cops who was sitting in a seat the overlooked the outfield. He walked down and sat beside the man. "Damn, the game ain't for another three days," he said. "You like to get here early."

The detective's name was Alphonso Callic, a thin black man with eighteen years on the force. He did not bother to look up from his clip board. "Hello, Inspector. How's life in the fast lane?"

"Slow. What are you working on these days?"

"Bullshit. Somebody broke into one of the vendors booths and took some cash. So says the owner of the booth. No proof either way."

"You think he wants a police report so he can claim it on his insurance?"

"The guy says he keeps fifty thousand in cash in the booth. What do you think?"

"That's a lot of hot dogs."

"Not at nine dollars apiece. Beer's the same. You can't bring your own. He'll get his money." Callic looked at O'Neil. "Word is you are working on some serious shit."

"Mum's the word and all that," O'Neil said. "Lots of rumors."

"Like rumors about two guys who want to blow this place up?" The detective was not smiling.

"Yeah, like that."

"Let me know if you need some help. One of the rumors has it that the task force handling this keeps losing the targets. You know anything about that?"

"Like I said, mum's the word. Just in case, what kind of help are you talking about?"

"Hey, Inspector, you got a lot of friends in the department. Just because the chief don't like you doesn't mean everybody else feels that way. Here's my card. Nobody wants to see this place blown up. Call me and I can get some guys to pitch in. No questions asked."

"Ask around if anyone has heard anything about the theft of things that make explosives. Maybe some of the homeless guys have run across somebody who's a little odd. Anything."

"Jesus, Inspector. Everybody on the street is odd. I'll ask around. Call me if you need some folks who know the streets and won't lose people." Callic winked.

"I need to get back to the department," O'Neil said. "Working for the feds is another world."

"So I heard." Callic got up and offered his hand. "Gotta go file this report. Keep in touch."

Gant waved O'Neil up to the mezzanine level. "Who was that?"

"An old friend from the department," he said.

"Can he help us?"

"Maybe. He offered. Something to consider."

"Set up a meeting with anyone on the D.C. department you think can help us."

"It will have to be off the books. The Chief's a stickler for rules."

"Whatever it takes."

Chapter Thirty-Five

Maskhadov and Ghazali drove into Shepardstown, West Virginia to find a shop that could quickly make a magnetic sign that could be affixed to the driver's side of the van they had stolen. The sign would bear the name and logo of the Finnegan Brothers Wholesale Supply, a Washington-based meat and produce supplier in business since 1933. The company's logo was a smiling pig in a tuxedo riding a hot dog. Maskhadov and Ghazali found the image offensive and disgusting.

Finnegan Brothers Wholesale Supply delivered hot dogs and sausages to a vendor at Nationals Park. Some weeks the numbers topped twenty thousand. The vendor, Dogs A Hittin', was popular with fans because it occasionally offered half-price nights that created long lines of grateful parents whose offspring demanded hot dogs along with the game.

Maskhadov had scouted the vendors at the park and knew which ones received large and frequent deliveries. He wore a rent-a-cop uniform into the park, hat down over his eyes, large glasses, and he waited until the early hours, when the park was empty of all but security and maintenance personnel. He broke into the vendor's booth to steal any document he could find that had the invoice from Finnegan Brothers to Dogs A Hittin'. He found what he needed in an unlocked drawer along with ten thousand dollars in cash. When the owner discovered the cash missing he called police and inflated the loss. He did not mention, nor did he notice, that several invoices were missing.

Maskhadov and Ghazali found a sign shop on a side street and presented themselves as contractors who needed a sign in a hurry. The young man behind the counter looked at the men, at the logo and company name, and said, "Two days."

"How much," Maskhadov asked.

"Two hundred. One-ninety if it's cash." The young man looked bored and waited for an answer.

"Three hundred cash if it's one day," Maskhadov said. "We want to make a good impression and get to work early."

The young man showed something that looked like a smile. "Ten o'clock tomorrow. I'll need payment now."

Maskhadov handed over the cash while the young man copied the logo from the invoice. "See you in the morning." He and Ghazali left Shepardstown and drove to Charles Town, where they checked into a cheap motel that catered to elderly men and women who were in town to play the slot machines and bet on the horse races at the casino and track. They paid in cash and no questions were asked.

***

It was not far from Charles Town to Winchester across the line in Virginia. The truck bore the name and logo of Finnegan Brothers Wholesale Supply. Maskhadov had altered the invoices to Dogs A Hittin' and now had three such invoices, all dated three and four days ahead. He and Ghazali went to a Wal-Mart and purchased green work shirts and pants, plus work boots and gloves.

The two men drove to the storage area where Ghazali had stashed the items and supplies. The van was heavy when the load was aboard and the weight caused Maskhadov to smile. *It is good.*

Ghazali was quiet as they drove to a strip of low-rent motels and checked in to a room that reeked of marijuana smoke and mold. They parked the truck away from the road and settled in to pray and reflect on their coming mission. Ghazali chose not to eat anything more in this life. He purchased several large bottles of juice.

Maskhadov was not preparing for Paradise. He believed that his missions on behalf of his hatred required him to send others to their reward or punishment. His reasoning was along the lines of practicality. How could he carry out more missions against the hated West if he were dead? Besides, he was not a man whose sexual tastes ran to virgins. His weakness was women of experience and willingness.

The van was not reported stolen for a day and a half. Virginia police typed its license plate number into a database. Most stolen vehicles are recovered by chance when an officer stops it for a traffic violation and types its plate into the database. The van was not on the streets and no one thought it unusual that a work van was parked behind a cheap motel.

***

Agent Patricia Gant and her task force reviewed images from Washington's hundreds of surveillance cameras. She refused to believe that the men they were seeking had left the city. The White House was refusing to go public with the search, even though rumors were in the air like so many bits of confetti. Gant thought it would be helpful to issue a public statement that Maskhodov and Ghazali were dangerous men being sought by the F.B.I. The publicity would put their photos on every television outlet and all over the Internet. Homeland Security objected to any public admission that the two men has slipped the knot twice and were planning to blow up Nationals Park during a game. Canceling the game was out of the question. The United States has the capability to deal with terrorists, so the reasoning went. There was no need to panic the city. Gant was again given new orders to find the fugitives and deal with them. The new orders did not forbid what the old hands referred to as "extreme prejudice."

***

Dave Haggard was lamenting his sobriety when O'Neil called. He was at a work station in the newsroom, looking for motivation to file a feature report for the weekend feed to the stations. All of his ideas were weak in a strict news sense. Reporters call them "evergreens" because they have no expiration date. He was working up an idea about how many tourists visit the Justice Department building on Constitution Avenue during the summer months. Justice was not a hot item on the tourist agenda. Kids from Omaha do not shout for Dad to take them to the Justice Department building. Air and Space, yes! Natural History, yes! Justice? What's that? Maybe he could make it a humor piece. God, he wanted a drink. Days of sobriety were taking their toll on his efforts to block out reality.

"Dave Haggard," he said.

"Hello, Scribe. It is I who serve and protect." O'Neil was in a jolly mood.

"What can I do for you, Inspector?"

"Aren't you supposed to remind me that the word scribe applies only to those who labor in print?"

"Don't have the energy. What's up?"

"Coffee shop. Fifteen minutes." O'Neil's voice had lost its jolliness.

The coffee shop was half-filled with Mellenials who had coffee cups in one hand and their smart phones in the other. O'Neil was at a back table when Dave walked in. "You could set fire to this place and nobody would notice," he said.

"What's up?" Dave had a pasty, unhealthy look.

"How long sober?" O'Neil had seen many men who were coming down from booze.

"Too long. Not long enough. Take your pick."

"Ah, the self-pity stage. It will pass. In the meantime, I have something you might like."

"Please tell me you've found these two guys and the threat is over."

"Not quite. We'd like you to put out a report using their names and photos and say they're being sought in connection with a planned terrorist attack on the East

Coast. Maybe that will shake loose somebody who's seen them."

"I thought I was supposed to keep all of this under wraps and wait for some kind of triumphal phone call."

"New plan."

"Meaning the old one fell apart and you have no idea where these guys are or what they're planning." Dave was sensing a great story and was already starting to write it.

"We have a good idea what they're planning. They want to blow up Nationals Park. We don't know when. We don't know where they are. We want to flush them out."

"Do you have photos?"

O'Neil pulled an envelope out of his coat pocket and handed it to Dave. "As good as we have."

"When did you last lose them?"

"Can't say. Let's leave it at we're are seeking the public's help in finding them."

"Is everybody on board with this?"

"Let's classify this as coming from a source close to the investigation, so, no, it's not official."

"How long until they trace it back to you?"

"By now half the city's anti-terrorist folks are either working it or know about it, so it's lots of people to look at."

"But not many who are known to meet with me."

"Okay, it's me, Gant, Ossening and Taylor, plus any ringers you talk to that I don't know about. They won't take the time to administer lie detectors until it's over and by then the ass covering will be in full bloom, so maybe they'll drop it. I can say this. Whatever we're doing right now ain't working."

Dave gave O'Neil a quick salute and walked back to Now News. Six hours later the photos of Maskhadov and Ghazali were on every television and computer screen in America, crediting Now News with breaking the story that a major terrorist attack was planned for the East Coast. A young man at a cheap motel front desk saw the faces and turned to a friend with whom he was sharing a joint. "How are you supposed to tell these people apart? I had a couple of guys in here who looked just like that. Shit, these guys all look alike." He turned off the television and never gave it another thought.

Chapter Thirty-Six

Maskhanov wore his oversized eyeglasses and his green workman's uniform to a Wal-Mart where he bought reading glasses for Ghazali. The glasses made Ghazali's eyes appear large and distracted from the rest of his face, making him less likely to be recognized on the street. The men left the motel where they had been staying and moved to one that was even seedier. This one was favored by illegals from Central America, who lived four to a room. Two more men with straight black hair driving a work van were not noticed.

The contents of the van were divided into fours, packaged, and placed atop four small creepers, the kind used by mechanics to slide under cars. The creepers have a flat area supported by small wheels and can function as dollies for other loads. The creepers made the four packages in the van easily portable.

Maskhadov bought a newspaper to check the National's schedule. The team was tied with Atlanta for first place in the Eastern Division. Every game was a sellout. The next home series, the last of the season was a three-game weekend stand. It was against Los Angeles, a team also fighting for a spot in the playoffs. The series would draw national attention. The Saturday night game was to be broadcast around the country as the Game of the Week. It was time to show the infidels how weak and powerless they are, Maskhadov thought, as he stared at his image in bathroom mirror. *We are not weak. We are not stooges of the West. We have suffered long enough.*

Ghazali was on his prayer rug, muttering what he had learned at the madras. Maskadov pitied him. *Those who believe as he believes are fools. The dead cannot know the peace that comes with bringing suffering to your enemy. The dead are dead.*

The series against Los Angeles began on Friday night. But that game was not going to be broadcast across America. The men would wait another day, until Saturday. Three days. Three days to wait and prepare. Ghazali drank his juice and prayed, speaking very little. Maskhadov watched television and laughed at the cable commentators shouting nonsense about American politics. He ate from vending machines and drank water from the sink. He exercised twice a day but without any serious effort. Ghazali appeared to be in a trance.

The room contained two beds. Ghazali believed he was living his final hours in this life and chose to forego comfort, so he slept on the floor, on a carpet that was stained and smelled of other people's sin.

Maskhadov relieved his boredom and tension by relieving his sexual energy and was often behind the closed bathroom door. He made no effort to hide what he was doing, which drove Ghazali deeper into his trance as he sought relief from his disgust.

On Friday night, as Maskhadov and Ghazali were making final preparations, a fight broke out in an adjoining room. A middle aged man and woman had checked in at mid-afternoon and loudly expressed their passion with moans and shouts that assaulted the senses of the two Muslims who were trying to find quiet to prepare for the slaughter they were planning. At some point the couple took a break and a sense of peace arrived.

At dusk there was a pounding on the door of the room where the couple were now sleeping and it grew louder until a shotgun blast opened the door. The husband of the woman had discovered the tryst and was determined to take his revenge.

Maskhadov stood in the doorway and watched as the couple tried to reason with the woman's husband, who was red-faced and waving the shotgun. He wondered why the other man would want to have sex with such a fat, ugly woman. The man was no prize, either. Both were dull-faced and had missing teeth. The husband began to pound his wife's lover with the barrel of the shotgun, using it as a club. Doors to other rooms opened and the fight became a spectacle, with men and women cheering for one man or the other. Maskhadov found it entertaining and told himself that people of such low quality did not deserve to take up space on Earth.

The sound of sirens broke into the cheering, hollering and screaming that was filling the air in the parking lot. Two police cars appeared with their lights flashing. Four officers jumped out of their patrol cars waving nightsticks and bullhorns, ordering everyone to clear the scene. Two of the officers waded into the fight and pulled the shotgun from the angry husband, pushing him to the pavement and ordering him to be quiet. The wife's lover was bleeding from his head and sat down in a daze. The woman was trying to kick her husband but was held back by one of the officers. Maskhadov found it very amusing.

"Everybody back to your rooms," an officer shouted. "Nothing to see here." The spectators who had been enjoying the show slowly moved away and stood in the doorways to the rooms to see what would happen next. The husband was handcuffed and led to one of the patrol cars. The bleeding lover was tended to by an EMS crew that was called in by the officers. Order was restored.

One of the officers saw Maskhadov standing in the door to his room and stared at him. He whispered something to another officer and went to his patrol car where he used the radio. He spoke into his handset and looked at Maskhadov, who realized he had spent too much time watching the fight. He went inside the told Ghazali to prepare to leave. Both men kept their small bags packed in case flight became necessary and they stood in the doorway hoping for a chance to run.

The woman whose husband was in custody ran to the patrol car where he sat and pounded on the window, shouting that he was a no good bastard and that she loved the bleeding man whose head was being bandaged. The husband shouted back and began rocking in the car, causing it bounce up and down. All four officers went to the woman to calm her down. When one of them put his hand on her shoulder, she turned and head-butted him, knocking him down. This caused the other officers to pounce on her and push her down. That produced a melee as the bleeding lover ran to the rescue of the woman he had been with in the motel room all afternoon.

Maskhadov turned to Ghazali. "Now. Go!" The two men ran to the van and raced out of the parking lot and onto the highway, where they headed west to the first intersection they came to, took a right, then a left, and weaved through rural roads until they were lost and assumed that the police were as confused about their location as they were.

**

Patricia Gants' team was alerted within an hour of the sighting at the motel and teams of agents were racing to the scene, sirens howling and lights flashing. They arrived at the motel parking lot in something resembling a law enforcement circus of noise, orders and guns drawn. Many of the residents of the motel assumed it was an immigration raid and they ran in all directions while Gant and her agents looked on.

"Goddam it, after them!" she shouted, waving her arms at the fleeing men and women.

"That's not them," an officer hollered. "They ain't nothin' but migrants. The ones you want already took off." The officer was one of the cops who broke up the fight. "No need to chase anyone from here." He shook his head. "These folks are pitiful," he said to another officer, who was watching the spectacle.

Gant grabbed a bullhorn and aimed it at her agents. "Stop! Back to the cars for a briefing." It took what to her seemed like a long time to regain some control. A couple of her agents returned to the cars with people who had been handcuffed. "Let them go," she said. "We don't have time to process them." There was grumbling but the captured were freed and took off down the highway.

She turned to the local cops. "Who knows what the hell happened here?"

An officer raised his hand. "We got a call about a domestic dispute. I saw a man I recognized as one of the men you're looking for and called it in."

"Was there one man or two?" She held up two photographs.

"At first, only one, but then I saw another guy in the room. We had to break up a fight and both of them took off in a van. By the time we could go after them they were gone."

"Did it occur to you that capturing these men was more important than breaking up a fight?" Gant asked.

"Not at the time, no. People were being hurt."

"If we don't catch these two a lot more people will be hurt." Gant used an F.B.I. radio to contact the operations desk at the Hoover Building to report what had been seen and what had happened. She was assured that a helicopter would be over the air within an hour. "Damn! Another hour and these two could be anywhere."

Chapter Thirty-Seven

Maskhadov and Ghazali were in West Virginia, although they didn't know it. What they knew was rural, winding roads through mountains. The roads linked small communities where the speed limit was twenty-five. Men and women sat on porches and watched the traffic, noting who was a neighbor and who was a stranger. The van with two swarthy men caused a few of them to remark that it must be harvest time because the Mexicans were back.

They crossed the South Branch of the Potomac River and came to the community of Springfield, where they saw a sign for a wildlife management area. A two lane highway brought them to a turnoff onto a gravel road that was designated as private for staff only. They slowly drove up to an area thick with trees and underbrush. Maskadov backed the van into a verdant spot and ordered Ghazali out of the vehicle.

"We must cover the van," he said. "We will camp here tonight."

Ghazali was dull-eyed and went through the motions of gathering evergreen branches to place against the van.

He did not speak to Maskhadov, he only muttered his prayers and imagined himself transporting to Paradise.

At dusk the forest was quiet except for the sounds of people going about their lives some distance from where the men were hiding. At one point there was the sound of a helicopter overhead, but it did not linger and seemed to be following the paved road. Sometime after midnight a police siren screamed up the road but it passed without stopping near the men in the woods.

***

Maskhadov spent a restless night, his mind going over his plans and what he would need to do to escape the trap that he knew was being set for him. He considered dealing with Ghazali and leaving him for the animals but the man had slipped into harmlessness and might be useful as the day passed and night fell in Washington.

Ghazali did not eat or drink. He emptied his bowels near the van and did not bother to cover it up, prompting Maskhadov to call him disgusting. At dawn Maskhadov ate raisins and yogurt, washed down with bottled water. He felt strong.

His plan was for the men to arrive at Nationals Park at mid-afternoon as supplies were being delivered to vendors before the game. The two would blend in to the pre-game activity at the park. Timing would determine success or failure. Leave the forest too early and they would be on the road and exposed for hours. Leave too late and they would miss their chance to fade into the day's deliveries. He did not know where they were, so he had no idea how long it would take them to drive to Washington. Nei-

ther man had a cell phone, phones were tracked and monitored and were dangerous.

He searched the van and found an old folded map of
Virginia under a pile of small tools in the glove compartment. The map was torn where it had been folded, so
some detail was missing. Maskhadov traced their route to
Winchester and tried to estimate which direction they had
travelled from there. The map included a portion of eastern West Virginia and, at the edge, he found the community of Springfield. He ran his finger in a line to Route 50
and then east to Winchester and Washington and estimat-
ed his travel time at three to four hours. They must leave
at mid-morning.

***

Gant's agents and local police spent the night searching the back roads in a wide area of Virginia and West
Virginia, from the suburbs of Washington to the wild
country along the Cacapon River and the South Fork of
the Potomac. The Hoover Building would offer only one
helicopter, claiming others were needed to patrol the skies
above Washington. The military offered air support but
not for twenty-four hours, even though Gant had stressed
that whatever horrible act was being planned would have
been accomplished by then.

Every dark-skin man with black hair who was seen
was stopped and interrogated. People who lived in the
hamlets along the highways had differing stories, some
saying they had seen the very men in the photos, others
saying all Mexicans looked alike and they could not pick
one from another, but, yes, a few had passed by in the

past day or so. The eye witness reports had the suspects in several places at the same time, and so were useless.

At dawn on Saturday Gant called her agents to a meeting at a firehouse in Springfield. "I know everyone is tired and frustrated. We would all like a little time off to get some sleep and clear our heads. We don't have time. We believe a move will be made in the next day or two and we can't take a break. Does anyone have anything solid? I'm not interested in theories or some story you got from a guy who lives in the woods. Do any of you have any credible sightings of these men?"

The agents looked around, hoping that one of them would raise his or her hand and offer something that would give this search an end. No one did. A senior agent named Ferguson, a man who had spent his career in the field, raised his hands.

"Yes?" Gant said, a hopeful look in her eye.

"May I suggest that we establish a perimeter closer to the assumed target? That way we could let them come to us."

Gant smiled. "My thoughts exactly. Let's get the hell out of here."

***

The agents formed a small convoy along Route 50 and headed back to Washington. An hour later a white van made the same journey. It was Saturday, so traffic was tolerable even when they reached the Capital Beltway and headed east to Interstate 395 north, which crosses into D.C. over the 14th Street bridge within sight of Nationals

Park. They stayed on the Southeast Freeway and exited at South Capitol Street, blocks from their destination.

Tourists walked and gawked with their cameras and new sandals. Locals jogged. Melennials sat in the sunshine at outdoor cafes and smiled at each other. A peaceful, beautiful day in a world-class city.

Chapter Thirty-Eight

Dave Haggard spent the morning at Now News, reading the wires and trying to distract himself. He wanted a drink. He wanted ten drinks. He had no interest in jogging on the Mall or playing softball on one of the fields near the Lincoln Memorial, where office teams ran off their fat and waited for their games to end so they could repair to a watering hole and drink beer all afternoon. He had no interest in sitting near the fountain at Dupont Circle and watching young women in summer dresses.

He longed for a break from the desire to be someone else, someone who did not ache for the burn of Tennessee whiskey down his throat and the sweet senselessness that followed. He accepted that he was a drunk, a lush. He had seen many talented and good reporters drink themselves out of the business and he didn't want to be one of them. He also knew a few who had overcome their addiction and functioned as normal people, although one or two had confessed to a longing for a drink after years of sobriety. One day at a time, they said. Right now, he was struggling with one minute at a time.

The wires had nothing new for him. Everything awful situation was still awful. The Middle East remained as it had been for a thousand years. Hatred and death. Poor black Americans were still looking up at the American dream. A few more shootings in a few American cities. Politicians were still idiots whose vision ended in the mirror. He had become like the journalists he despised, bitter and cynical.

It occurred to him that the old drunks at the Press Club were only showing him the way forward, the life that a career of being lied to by public officials inevitably produced, a general feeling that it's all bullshit, so who cares. Nobody. That was his mood when his phone rang.

"Dave Haggard," he said in a voice that was somewhere between asleep and despair.

"Bud Ossening. I'm in the coffee shop in the lobby." The phone went dead.

Dave took the elevator and was in the lobby in less than two minutes. No one else was in the building and the elevator was an express straight down. Ossening was in casual clothes, khakis, polo shirt, running shoes and a Baltimore Orioles cap.

"Orioles?" Dave said, offering his hand.

"Cal Ripken was my hero. What can I say?"

"To what do I owe this honor?"

"Tonight, we think," Ossening said, raising his eyebrows.

"How do you know?"

"I said think, not know. Gant and her agents have set up a command post at a construction site near the park. You may want to make yourself available."

"Any other reporters being alerted?"

"Not that I'm aware of."

"Is she there now?"

"I can give you a ride."

***

Ossening was driving his private vehicle, an SUV with a child safety seat in the back. Fast food wrappers were on the floor. Dave had never seen the personal side of the agent.

"So, Dave, I hear rumors that you have a problem with alcohol. Any truth in that?"

"Some, yes," Dave said. "How'd you know about that?"

"I hear things. I don't have to tell you that people with that kind of problem sometimes let their mouths run a little too much."

"I haven't said anything to anybody. I don't socialize much."

"Did you tell your boss?"

"Of course. He's not the type to share information."

"All this stuff matters, Dave." Ossening kept his eyes straight ahead down Constitution Avenue. Dave watched the tourists at the Vietnam Veterans Memorial. "You ever been to the Wall?"

"Yes," Ossening said, "my dad's name is on it."

"I'm sorry," Dave said.

"No problem. I was too young to know him."

The two rode past the Washington Monument, the museums, and government buildings, including the Justice Department. Ossening saluted as he drove past, smiling. "All hail Justice," he said. He turned to Dave and smirked. "Nest of thieves."

He turned right near the Capitol and made his way to South Capitol Street and pulled into a large construction area near the ballpark. "They're in the trailer. I gotta get back."

Dave got out and watched as Ossening drove away. He didn't see the agent speak into a small microphone. "He's taken the bait," Ossening said.

Gant was waiting at the door of the trailer. She did not look happy to see Dave. "Well, well. Look who's here," she said. "I suppose we'll let you in. Everything is background. You know what that means."

"Maybe you should clarify," Dave said.

"Not one word of what you see, hear or read can be made public unless and until I clear it. Understood?"

"Got it."

The trailer was the office of the construction crew that was building a retail and condo complex as part of the new neighborhood going up around Nationals Park. At the moment it was nothing more than a large hole in the ground. All of Gant's agents were wearing hard hats. Gant was dressed in jeans and a loose man's shirt that hung over her belt and offered cover for the handgun she wore.

"I suppose you're wondering why we called you here," O'Neil said, hoping Dave would find the comment amusing. "We're all hoping the Nats make the playoffs tonight."

"Will somebody tell me what's happening?" Dave asked, looking at O'Neil and Gant.

"We think our bad guys will make their move tonight and we're here to cheer them on," O'Neil said. Gant and her agents were not amused.

"You may watch and stay out of the way," she said.

O'Neil stood up. "Here, put this on." He handed Dave a hard hat.

"You're kidding, right? I'd look ridiculous in that."

"You already look ridiculous. If you want me to show you around you'll have to wear this and some sunglasses," O'Neil said. "This guy Ghazali or Gutierrez or whatever he's calling himself knows what you look like. If he shows up and sees you he might wonder what you're doing here five hours before the game. The stadium isn't even open yet."

Dave put on the hat and hoped he didn't look as foolish as he felt. O'Neil opened the door to the trailer and looked around. To Dave he looked like an out-of-shape middle-aged cop trying to pass as a construction worker. The two men walked through an opening in the chain link fence that protected the site and headed away from the stadium.

"We've got a perimeter set up by zones. Zone one is closest to the stadium. Zone two is two blocks away. Zone three is three blocks. Cameras are on the rooftops along with some D.C. sniper types and a few specialized feds. Some of Congressman Taylor's friends are in the mix, scanning the people who are coming to the game. There's no way these two doers can penetrate security we have here."

"Why me?"

"You've been in on this from the beginning. I told Gant you should be here when it ends."

"And what's in it for you?"

"Why does there have to be something for me?"

"Call me cynical. I've been around this kind of thing before. As they say in country music, this ain't my first rodeo."

"There's too much bullshit in this town, Dave. When this is over, if it goes well, everything swinging dick in the city will claim credit. If it goes south, Gant takes the fall, with me strapped to her back. We need somebody who can take it from A to Z. Can we trust you to do it?"

"How does Gant feel about all of this?"

"Not good. She hates your kind."

"My kind?"

"Reporter types. She doesn't trust you but she's willing to see how this goes. She's a very smart woman, Dave. Let me say this. If you screw her your life will never be the same."

"I think you told me that once."

"Several times. We have a history."

"That was a long time ago," Dave said.

"Play by the rules, Dave."

Chapter Thirty-Nine

Maskhadov and Ghazali were in a white van bearing a magnetic sign with the name of a food supply company that was well-known at Nationals Park. It was one of more than a dozen white vans bearing signs of businesses that supplied the park with food, toilet paper, cups, and thousands of other items that forty-thousand men, women and children need or consume during the course of a three-hour baseball game. The vans, along with bigger trucks, came and went in boring repetition over the long season.

Police officers who routinely moved traffic and pedestrians no longer paid attention to the vendor vans arriving hours before the first pitch. The extra security Agent Gant had put in place made spot checks of all vehicles and scanned pedestrians, but even well before game time it was not possible to check everyone. Agents had memorized the photos of Maskadov and Ghazali and were relying on facial recognition software to find the men if they slipped through the visual checks.

The van carrying the two men was slowed at an intersection two blocks from the stadium. A D.C. cop raised her hand and walked to the driver's door. "State your business," she said.

Maskhadov handed her one of the invoices he had created. He tried to look and sound bored. "Delivery," he said.

The officer glanced at the invoice, saw that it was an everyday delivery, and waved him on. An F.B.I. agent a block away saw the van being waved through and assumed that it had been cleared, so he ignored the van as it passed him.

Maskhadov drove to a loading dock and waited until a stadium worker waved him to a spot where he could back in and unload. The dock was busy with suppliers hauling boxes on dollies and motorized carts. The game would produce great thirst and hunger, and a desire for caps, shirts and trinkets.

He opened the rear doors of the van and removed a dolly that was attached to a side panel. The four boxes inside the van's cargo area were plain cardboard sealed with gray gaffer tape. Maskhadov had hand-printed THIS SIDE UP on the boxes to make it appear as though something fragile was inside. He wore his workers uniform, cap, and large glasses. He wore fake sideburns to alter the contours of his face in the event he was seen on cameras attached to facial recognition software.

Ghazali was in a dream-like state, only partially aware of his surroundings. He did not know whether he had ascended to Paradise or to some other state of being. He glanced at Maskhadov and did not recognize him. He saw a man who appeared to be evil, at least in his present state. Maskhadov's face was covered with hair and glasses and Ghazali imagined that the man was Satan trying to disguise himself.

Ghazali looked around to see if anyone was on fire or showing signs of living in Hell, but all he saw were men and women hauling boxes or other containers into the bowels of the stadium. He looked again at Maskhadov and experienced a moment of panic. *How could they not know this man was Satan? Am I the only one who has the true vision?* Satan motioned for Ghazali to help him unload the van. His breathing became loud and fast. He thought he heard the voice of Allah telling him to kill Satan. He looked for the source of the voice but it was only a man on the dock yelling that they were killing time.

He calmed himself and promised that he would strike Satan when he had the opportunity. Until then, he would act as he was told. He moved to Maskhadov and helped unload a box.

Maskhadov had designated four areas of the stadium for the boxes. Each was near a support pillar and away from foot traffic. The two men spent half an hour going about their task, leaving the boxes in out-of-the-way spots and placing other items on the boxes to make it appear as though they had been there awhile. One box was covered with a mop and broom, another with a plastic bag filled with cardboard tubes from paper towel dispensers, things that were left to be disposed of.

He and Ghazali returned to the van where he tested the signals that controlled the packages. All was in order. The only loose end was Ghazali. He would die tonight, Maskhadov had no doubt about that. But he had wired the packages to respond to his radio command from a quarter-mile away, so there was no need for Ghazali to remain at the stadium and begin his journey to Paradise there. Maskhadov considered sending the man to his reward immediately and solving the problem of what to do with him.

Ghazali was having some thoughts of his own. He could not remember what had happened to the handgun he'd carried until the two men holed up at the motel in Frederick. He could not recall giving it to Maskhadov nor did he remember disposing of it in any other way. He checked his pants and did not find the weapon.

"I need to get something from the van," he said.

"What do you need?" Maskhadov was concerned that Ghazali was going crazy.

"It's personal for me," Ghazali said.

"What is it?"

"I do not ask you what you are doing. It is personal. It is for me." Ghazali was agitated.

"I'll go with you."

"If I go to relieve myself will you follow and watch? I can do what I want and I do not need you to be my father." Ghazali stormed off and sped down a flight of stairs to the loading area.

Maskhadov watched him and let him go. *Maybe he will fall down and kill himself.*

The van had been left at the loading dock where other suppliers were waiting to unload and take supplies to vendors. A stadium supervisor was waiting by the van. "Where have you been? Do you see the other trucks? They need to unload. Get this thing out of here."

"We must remain for awhile. Where may I park it?" Ghazali used his Spanish accent and appeared to be humble and apologetic.

"Ah, shit," the supervisor said. "Over there by the fence."

Ghazali moved the van and backed it against a portion of a fence that was hidden from public view. He opened the glove box and found only papers. He looked under the seats and found only old trash. He searched the cargo area and discovered the handgun hidden in a small well where tools needed to change the tires were kept. The weapon was wrapped in a motel towel that was damp. Ghazali unwrapped it and found that the gun was rusting but appeared to be functional. He checked the chamber and saw that the round there was not rusty or gritty. He removed the round and checked the barrel, finding only specks of dust.

He re-chambered the round and slipped the gun into his beltline at his back. His loose shirt covered it. He smiled. Satan must be sent back to Hell. He remained in the cargo area of the van and prayed, positioning his head facing east. He felt better. His head was clear. He remembered why he was at the stadium and what he had to do. He believed that he would know when to strike Satan. He found a bottle of juice and drank it.

Chapter Forty

Congressman Peter Taylor sat in his office and fumed. *Bozos! That's what they are. Bozos who have no idea how to make it happen. Clowns.* It all came down to training and professionalism. *These guys don't have it,* he thought, rubbing his face. It was an old habit when he was agitated. Taylor, like many military intelligence types, believed that the F.B.I. was nothing more than a gang of ego-driven cops who longed for the days when they could chase communists and John Dillinger. Chasing terrorists, real bad guys, was best left to the pros.

Taylor was incensed that this woman, Patricia Gant, was running the operation to root out Maskhadov and Ghazali. She had no record to speak of, at least in a special operations sense. Her dog runner, an Army term for aide de camp, was a disgraced cop. Amateurs.

Taylor had learned that his communications were being captured on orders of the Chairman of the Intelligence Committee, who was threatening to bring him up on ethics charges because he had kept the Committee in the dark regarding the information he had on Maskhadov and Ghazali. The Chairman had also suggested that sharing classified information with Dave Haggard was tantamount to treason.

He could not contact his people on either his office or his cell phone, nor could he text or email without getting a call from the Chairman wanting a full briefing on what he was doing. He was probably being followed, possibly by the F.B.I. *Wouldn't that be a kick.*

He had alternatives. He got up from his desk and told his legislative aide that he was leaving for the day. The woman was a veteran committee staffer who had been foisted on him by the Chairman and he knew she would report everything he did in the office.

"You have a four o'clock with the Knoxville Chamber of Commerce," she said.

"You meet with them. Tell them a serious national security issue has come up and I was called away to a very important meeting. Then tell them how hard I am working on issues that are important to them. Standard stroking. I know you can handle it." He smiled his most engaging smile, showing perfect teeth, and walked out into the hallway. The aide could hear his shoes fall onto the marble floor all the way to the elevator. She dialed the Chairman's office and whispered, "He's leaving."

Taylor walked out onto Independence Avenue and looked north to see the great dome of the Capitol gleaming in the afternoon sun. He tried to summon the ghosts of the great ones but all he felt was a sadness.

Tourist busses disgorged those who still felt the magic and watched them take photos of each other with the Capitol in the background. He walked west down to the Mall and into the Museum of the American Indian on

Third Street Southwest. He walked through an atrium where large cutout canoes were on display, past the gift shop, and into the café where so-called Native American food was served, mostly Indian-themed burgers and other common items that white people eat. He found a table in a far corner, sat, and pretended to be absorbed by his phone. He looked for signs that he was being followed. If he was, they were good, he thought. He didn't spot a tail.

He went to the gift shop and bought a shirt and hat with the museum's logo. He went to the rest room and removed his suit jacket and dress shirt, replacing them with his purchases. He lifted a ceiling tile and deposited his coat and shirt. He would retrieve them later. After all, they were very expensive.

He used an exit to the Mall and fell in with a tourist group that was walking to the Air and Space Museum next door. The museum is the most popular spot on the Mall and is crowded every day of the tourist season. The first floor was packed with kids, parents, and Japanese tourists who photographed everything in all directions, snapping shots of the planes hanging from the ceiling and the rockets soaring up from the floor. He made his way to a back door and exited, hailing a cab that was dropping off a family from the Heartland.

He paid the cabbie twenty-dollars to drive him one block to the Smithsonian Metro station, where he caught the Silver Line to Tysons Corner. It was mid-afternoon. The train was crowded but not packed as it would be during the evening rush. He wore his tourist hat and shirt and endured the glances of the regulars who never wore anything that smacked of Washington, D.C. or any local landmark not associated with a sports team.

He kept his head down and appeared to be focused on his phone, as were most of the others on the train. He exited at Tysons Corner and doubled back to catch an inbound train that would take him to Mclean. He did not see anyone mirroring his movements and again assumed that he was not being tailed or—if he was—they were very good.

He got off in Mclean and walked to a convenience store, where he bought a prepaid cell phone and dialed a number. It answered with a slight click. He whispered a coded address, ended the call, and stomped on the phone, tossing it into a dumpster behind the store.

Fifteen minutes later a Mercedes sedan pulled up to a stop sign on Dolly Madison Boulevard and Taylor climbed into the passenger seat. No words were exchanged. In Mclean, a Mercedes is considered basic transportation and draws no unwanted attention. The car drove to a residential neighborhood overlooking the Potomac River and the George Washington Memorial Parkway. The view of the falls was spectacular. Taylor was not there for the sights.

He walked to a well-tended lawn facing the river and found two men sitting in the sun, drinking German beer. "Hello, Peter, pull up a glass." The man speaking was a section chief at the Defense Intelligence Agency named Ahmed Tavana, formerly of Iran's intelligence service. Tavana was a well-educated speaker of a dozen languages whose grasp of the world was not burdened by morality, which he considered sentimental nonsense.

"Hello, Ahmed. Don't mind if I do," Taylor said, lowering himself into an Adirondack chair.

"You know, the Germans still make the best beer and I don't care what these fancy new brewers say. You can't argue with five hundred years of excellence." He held up his glass and took a deep pull. "Damn, nothing like it on a warm afternoon."

"As much as I would like to discuss beer, I'm afraid I'm here for some information that will cheer me," Taylor said.

"The news is not good, my friend," Tavana said. "There is a lot of activity at Nationals Park but we don't see results. It could be real or just another fuckup, if you will pardon my crassness."

"I have the Chairman up my ass."

"I know. We monitor your calls, too." Tavana said. "And others."

"What does the Chairman know?"

"What everybody knows. Two guys are planning something and we're all running around like little mice trying to find out what it is and stop it."

"We know what it is."

"We think we know. There's a difference." Tavana stopped talking while a waiter brought a tall glass of beer to Taylor.

"Let's say we know the players, these guys Maskhadov and Ghazali. Let's assume they didn't just come up with this idea and buy a plane ticket to America. Where does this go?" Taylor looked at Tavana and took a long pull on the glass.

"Who knows? Maybe al qaeda, maybe ISIS, maybe Iran. These days, they're breed like rabbits."

"Do you think your old colleagues are capable of something like this?" Taylor said.

"My old colleagues are capable of anything in all senses. They have the resources, the knowledge, the means and, in their minds, the motivation. But I don't think it's them. Blowing something up in Washington is not their style. They don't want to create a short term disaster. They have long-term plans, like blowing up the entire Western World. No, I think we're looking at some group, probably in Pakistan, who want to kill lots of Americans on American soil and crow about it to increase their funding."

The third man in the group, the one who was talking with Tavana when Taylor arrived, raised his hand. "If I may. Who gives a shit right now who's behind this. If we can't stop it, they win and we look like fools. The other side doesn't care that we have the best military or the latest technical tools. They're beating us by going back to the 1960s."

"We're not beaten yet, Mr. Director," Tavana said.

"Yeah? Remind me of that later." The Director stood up and shook hands with Tavana and Taylor. "Congressman, why don't you quit the House and find real work. Now, if you will excuse me, I'm needed down the road in Langley, where people know what they're doing."

"Mr. Director, are your people on this? Can you stop it?"

"No comment." The Director went to his car.

Forty-One

Dave and O'Neil walked the stadium, past the food and the souvenirs, upper and lower levels. The field was immaculate. Grounds crews were raking the infield. The concourses were swept and scrubbed. Ushers were gathered in small groups to chat about baseball and life in general. Well over two million fans had seen games in the stadium over the season. The stadium had changed the neighborhood. It was all bright and shiny and new. New condos and offices. New bars and restaurants. New attitudes about life near the Navy Yard.

"Unbelievable," Dave said, waving his arm in the direction of the field.

"If you had been here thirty years ago you would have seen a whole other city," O'Neil said. "Shabby, hopeless, and full of junkies and hookers. Right on this block. Now look at it."

"Do you think the threat is real here?" Dave said.

"Me? Yes. Some people live short miserable lives in terrible places and they don't like people who live long wonderful lives in other places. Hatred and envy are strong motivators, Dave. So, yes, I think there are people who would like nothing better than to blow us all to kingdom come."

"Tonight?"

"Maybe." O'Neil stopped a stadium security guard. "Anything out of the ordinary?"

"Nothing except all you people askin' if anything's out of the ordinary," the guard said.

"Thanks for taking it seriously," O'Neil said, walking away from the man.

"It's a baseball game. It ain't Iraq," the guard said, shaking his head.

Dave and O'Neil spent an hour walking the stadium, from the upper decks to the loading docks. Nothing appeared to be out of place, although O'Neil made a note to have the custodians clean up the out-of-the-way areas that to him appeared to be used as storage areas. He saw boxes covered in cleaning supplies and considered calling the Fire Marshall to ask whether they were a fire hazard. *Probably not,* he thought. The place was concrete and steel and couldn't burn.

F.B.I. agents went into the vendors' booths and checked behind stoves and counters, looking for suspicious packages. Dogs sniffed the booths and the seating areas but not the loading area, which was crowded with trucks, dollies, men and women, all hurrying. A decision was made to check the supplies at their delivery points, not on the docks.

Maskhadov busied himself by acting as though he was counting something, walking from booth to booth, writing down numbers. He was wearing his work clothing and hat pulled low over his face. He gave wide berth to the sniffer dogs, presenting himself as a man afraid of dogs. He noted security points and counted the police and agents who were searching the booths. He briefly thought of blowing up the stadium before the game just to get it over with.

He had lost track of Ghazali, which made him nervous. Ghazali was unstable in his religious visions. He could lose his focus on the mission. It would be a disaster if the man went mad before the mission could succeed.

Ghazali was crouched behind the van near the fence. He had an urge to shoot someone. He didn't care who. He fondled the handgun and checked again to see that a round was in the chamber. He imagined the bullet entering a human head and saw the blood and brains that would spew from the exit wound. He imagined that it was his head and saw himself floating toward Paradise in bliss. It was just a finger pull away. But suicide with no martyrdom was the path to Hell, not Paradise, and Satan himself was here in the stadium, waiting to pull him into the fires of eternity.

No, he must deal with Satan. And he remembered why he was at the stadium. Yes! He will be martyred when the infidels are destroyed. Tonight. It came back to him. He had two tasks, two final tasks, in this life. He must destroy Satan and he must carry out his mission. He put the handgun into his beltline at the base of his spine and stood up. He smiled. He would not see the sun rise tomorrow but would look down upon the pitiful Earth from his spot in Paradise, laughing at the poor fools who cling to this life.

He walked up the ramp to the loading area and into the heart of the stadium. He found his way to the upper section overlooking right field and climbed to the highest row where he walked to the end near a wall, where he found a seat and watched the stadium slowly come to life. He looked down upon groundskeepers, vendors, security forces and a few reporters who were preparing to cover the game. From the field, Ghazali appeared to be a stadium worker taking a break or just another security agent keeping an eye on things. He attracted no attention.

Maskhadov was on the move. He was jittery and anxious. He had lost track of Ghazali and feared that the man had lost his mind. He kept to the shaded areas on the concourses and carried a broom to throw off any random suspicion that he was without duties and therefore to be watched. When he saw someone looking at him he found a spot to sweep and even picked up odd bits of trash that suppliers had dropped. Time was slow and the moments hung in the air as he waited for the stadium to fill with fans.

Sunset was just before seven, ten minutes before the first pitch. He checked the stadium clock and saw that he had over two hours until darkness settled over the city. He felt sick to his stomach with fear. He was not a man to fear violence but he had no patience and his desire to act was overwhelming his reason. He went to a restroom and vomited, hoping it would ease his tension. It did not.

He walked to a railing overlooking home plate and glanced up at the stands. First, to left center field where a few early arrivals were lounging and drinking beer. He looked up at the restaurant where fans could dine and watch the game over center field. He scanned the upper sections and saw a lone man sitting as far from the field as was possible. He could barely make out the clothing the man was wearing but it appeared to match his own. *Ghazali!*

He had to get to him before the man could slip away again. He hurried along the concourse to the stairs that would take him up to the highest level. He could not run or he would be noticed, so he feigned an urgent stride, acting like a man with a broom who had an mess that must be cleaned up immediately. He did not make eye contact with anyone he passed. He did not stop. He made it to the second concourse and nearly ran to section 236, where he climbed the stairs to find that Ghazali was gone. He looked around and saw only ushers and security people.

Where was he? He asked an usher if he had a seen a man wearing the same clothing, explaining that the man he was looking for was a co-worker who was needed at the loading dock. The usher shook his head and went back to a conversation with another man.

Maskhadov slowly made his way down the stairs to the concourse and went to the railing to look down at the first level. It was his last vision in this life. A shot came from behind him, sending a bullet into his brain. He fell forward onto the seats below. The shot was loud but it blended in with other noises and the workers who were tossing containers and creating their own sounds were unaware that someone had been shot until shouts erupted when Maskhadov's body hit the seats on the lower concourse.

A security guard yelled that someone had fallen over the railing. Another guard ran to the body and saw Maskhadov's head mangled and bleeding and assumed that he had been injured in the fall. It was five minutes before an F.B.I. agent arrived and declared that the man had been shot in the head.

Agent Gant was in her trailer command post when the F.B.I. radios came to life. She and other agents ran the block to the centerfield entrance and saw that fans were steaming in to watch batting practice and eat hot dogs before the game. Her first thought was that it was too late to lock it down.

The section where Maskhadov's body lay was sealed from the public. Agents took photographs and forensics experts tested for whatever they could find. Curious onlookers took their own photographs with their smartphones and posted them on the Web, most saying that a man had fallen from the upper level.

Gant ordered a seal on the details and told stadium management that there had been an accident. By six o'clock Maskhadov's body had been taken away and cleanup crews were brought in to make the section presentable to the oncoming fans. Reporters were told that a man had fallen, was seriously injured, and had been taken to a hospital.

"Let's try to keep this thing from going into space," Gant said, addressing her task force. "The shooter is likely still here and planning to go through with whatever they planned. Find out how many places there are to hide and check them all. Make sure you're wearing body armor. This guy is serious."

Dave and O'Neil listened and watched as the agents spread out. "We're an hour from the first pitch," O'Neil said. "We're getting to maximum pucker time."

"Why did you guys lie to the media?" Dave asked.

"We need to keep it buttoned up. If we announce that some guy got shot then we have to declare the whole place a crime scene and cancel the game and that leads to other questions and before you know it we have a full scale panic and the cat's out of the bag."

"Inspector, the cat's already out. Half this town knows something is up."

"They don't know anything, Dave, they just pass rumors to each other."

"Sometimes those rumors are true."

"Spare me. Tell it to the tourists."

"It's going to come out, all of it. You know that."

"We want it to come out, Dave. Just not right now. When it does, you'll be the big dog."

"I feel pretty slimy right now, letting these false reports go out about the guy accidentally falling over the rail."

"You don't have a choice. Hang in there. Watch betting practice. Maybe you'll shag a ball."

Dave felt like a five year old who's been told to sit down and behave. He watched as the section where Maskhadov had fallen was opened to smiling fans carrying nine-dollar cans of beer.

Chapter Forty-Two

Ghazali was surprised that no one was chasing him. He had assumed that the killing of Satan would produce a hoard of satanic fanatics to come for him and he was prepared to martyr himself, but not without regrets for not having fulfilled his mission. He ran from the stadium toward the Anacostia River, stumbling through a construction zone that fronted on Potomac Avenue Southeast. He slowed and walked to Diamond Teague Park on the river and followed a metal ramp to a floating dock where a young woman was pulling kayaks out of the water.

"How much to rent?" he said in his Mexican accent.

"We're closing for the day," she said, with a sweet smile.

"I have money. Fifteen minutes. That is all. Please." He offered his most sincere smile.

The young woman offered a look of pity. "I have to leave in half an hour and all of these kayaks have to be locked up before I leave. I'm cleaning up now."

"Fifteen minutes. No more. I have money." He showed her a twenty-dollar bill.

"Stay close," she said. "I can't be late."

He paddled away from the dock and headed up river toward the Navy Yard. Strollers waved from the Anacostia Riverwalk Trail and he smiled and waved back. A futuristic walkway carried the strollers over water and on to another park, part of the massive redevelopment that had accompanied the constructions of the ballpark. It was a warm late-summer evening and everyone was happy. Everyone except Ghazali, who was in a frantic state and paddling fast.

He pulled the kayak into a spot along the seawall at the river's edge and jumped out, pushing the craft into the current and sending it downstream to the young woman, who was yelling something he couldn't hear. He walked past a restaurant that overlooked the river, unnoticed by the diners.

He did not want to go far from the stadium. His plan was to wait until the late innings, get back to the van and retrieve the electronic detonator and wait for the moment. Until then, he needed a place to hide.

A small two-story building was being demolished along a block that fronted the stadium. It's walls and floors had been removed but the concrete skeleton remained and was cluttered with construction equipment and a large dumpster. The dumpster was filled with boards, boxes, large buckets and other items of trash. He looked inside and saw empty spaces where items that had been tossed into the dumpster had rested on top of large chunks of wallboard or lumber.

He climbed inside and found a spot against the rear wall. He moved a few things and made himself a tiny cave. He closed his eyes and imagined his trip to Paradise and wondered if he would ascend in the smoke and screams from what was to come. He dozed in a dreamless state until cheering from the stadium woke him up.

***

In a booth high above the field Charlie Steiner was calling the game for Los Angeles. "Bottom of first. Game is tied at one on that home run by Washington. One out. We're looking at a sellout crowd in a game that's critical to both teams."

Ghazali could hear none of it. He slowly came around in the dark of the dumpster. His ass and his back hurt from the cramped space and the steel sides and bottom. A two-by-six had slipped and was pressing an exposed nail against his forehead. It hurt to move but he knew he must leave the dumpster to get about his mission. Getting up was hard for him. He had to move the construction trash that had settled onto him and he was cut by nails and sharp edges from the debris. His clothes were torn in several places. He would be noticed. He tried to think of an explanation and decided to say he had fallen should someone ask about his appearance.

He crossed South Capitol Street. A D.C. police officer was in the intersection to control pedestrians who were streaming into the stadium. She looked at his clothing and asked him if he was okay. He nodded and chuckled. "I fell down some stairs," he said in his Mexican accent. "I got too much work to do."

The officer laughed with him. "Your wife is gonna have something to say when you get home." She turned her attention to a hundred of so fans who were waiting to cross, waving them on.

Ghazali went around to the loading dock entrance and saw that it was quiet except for the drivers who were standing in small groups smoking and talking. He was not stopped when he walked into the area where trucks were parked. He drew a glance from a couple of security guards who were smoking on the dock but they did not question his appearance. He heard one of them whisper, "That's not the look management likes to see."

He went to the van and found it undisturbed. No one paid attention to him as he went to the rear of the vehicle and retrieved a small device that resembled a flashlight. The device had a lighted face that displayed numbers. There was a button at the top that, when pressed, would send a signal to the four boxes that were snuggled against the pillars in the stadium. He would need to key in a code to activate the button. Maskhadov had written the code on the device in the event that his mind went blank as the critical moment. He had no way of knowing that he would not be alive when the code was needed.

Ghazali's hands were shaking as he placed the device in a shirt pocket. He was not nervous about his ability or willingness to carry out the deed. He was thinking about Paradise and had a vision of the virgins he would be with in the moment the button on the detonator was pressed. He felt weak in the knees and sat on the bumper to regain his composure. He looked at the others on the dock and felt no connection to them. He was already in another place that was not of this world.

Chapter Forty-Three

The second inning was scoreless for both teams. Charlie Steiner's play by play was about pitching and batting statistics. All of the inning's batters for both teams went to three and two and fouled several times, drawing out the inning without sending anyone to the bases. Strikeouts and pop ups. The crowd was still filing in and buying beer, hot dogs and nachos before they found their seats. The stadium's on-scene reporter interviewed fans as they filed in and displayed the interviews on the giant screen. Kids wore their new hats. Middle-aged men wore team jerseys bearing the names of their favorite players. There were far more Washington fans than Los Angeles supporters, judging by the hats in the crowd. The evening was warm. Playoffs were on the line. The crowd was happy, even those high in the upper decks.

***

Gant was in her trailer, polling her agents about what they were seeing, which was nothing out of the ordinary. Their search for Ghazali had not turned up anything promising. Gant thought it was foolish not to cancel the game and clear the stadium. Her superiors disagreed and said everyone would look foolish if it was all for nothing. *We can't let terrorist threats control what we do*, they said. *If we do, they win.*

Gant thought it was irresponsible. *What will they say if this place blows up?* Her agents were told to keep moving through the crowd and watch for anything suspicious. She conceded that such instructions are empty to experienced agents but she wanted to reinforce the idea that somewhere in the crowd was the man they were hunting. He had already killed Maskhadov and he would not hesitate to kill again.

O'Neil returned to the trailer accompanied by Dave Haggard, who was not happy. "If it's all the same to you, I'd like to go back inside the watch the game," he said.

"Actually, no, it's not the same to me," Gant said. "We need to keep an eye on you to make sure you don't break the embargo, to use a journalism term."

"You mean file about all of this? What's to file? There have been all kinds of reports about security alerts and possible threats. What can I say? There's no news here."

"You're not selling me, Dave." Gant said

O'Neil sat on a folding chair and wiped the sweat off his face. "Hell, I'll go watch it with him. I'm not doing much."

"Stick around for awhile," Gant said. "Let's see what happens. The stadium will be at capacity in half an hour and we'll need all hands on deck."

"Has it occurred to you that this could turn out to be a giant clusterfuck?" O'Neil said. "We have a whole task force on this and not only does this guy make fools out of us all over the city he comes into the stadium under our noses and shoots and kills his partner. Not our finest hour."

"It's not over yet," Gant said. "We can find him first."

"Agent Gant," O'Neil said, using his formal cop voice, "This guy has killed his inside man on the electric grid scheme, he's eluded us twice and now he's here playing catch me if you can. This plan seems kind of weak."

"And your plan is what, Inspector?" Gant stared at O'Neil with a look of disgust,.

"I just thought you supercop types at the Bureau were better than this."

"Do you think D.C. police could have done any better?"

"I think D.C. police would have called off the game."

"To achieve what?"

Dave broke in. "Maybe you two should take this outside. You sound like an old married couple nagging each other over something that can't be changed. Agent Gant, I'm going to the goddam game and you can arrest me if you like." He stepped outside into the humid air and walked to the centerfield gate, where he was recognized by an agent and waved in.

He waved to Johnny Holliday, who was heading up to the press box after his pregame television show.

"What are you doing here?" Holliday said, offering his hand. "I saw that story you had about the terrorists. Nice going."

"Big game tonight," Dave said.

"Biggest of the season. Hey, enjoy the game." Holliday stepped onto an elevator that would take him to the press box.

Dave had no ticket and was not cleared for the press box, so he walked the lower concourse, grabbing a beer at a vendor known for its chili dogs. He grabbed one of those, too, and leaned against a post at the railing overlooking the field. The stands were packed with fans waving their hats and chanting. He tried to imagine a bomb in a place like that. What would it feel like? How many would die? He looked at the fans and saw kids with dads, office workers with friends, couples getting to know each other on first dates.

Washington lost two major league teams in the twentieth century, both named Senators, one to Minnesota and the other to Texas. Both owners claimed it was not a baseball town, yet over two million fans had filled the seats in the season that was ending, more than many other, older, baseball cities.

Dave had grown up in East Tennessee where baseball fans followed Atlanta. Atlanta was now in the same division as Washington, so he had switched allegiance. He knew the players and he went to games and told his friends that Nationals Park was the best in the league. He had to force himself to take the threat against the park seriously. How could such a thing be possible? He wanted to believe that the people in charge of the city's security would not allow it to happen. It would be as bad as 9/11. Who would we go to war against this time? How many lives would be affected in one way or another?

He lost his appetite and tossed the chili dog in a trash can, gulped his beer, and walked around the stadium with his press badge hanging around his neck. Some of Agent Gant's men and women recognized him and nodded. Stadium security stared at him but did not try to stop him.

Those who were searching for Ghazali wore serious cop faces and stood out from the happy fans enjoying the game. *Do they even suspect what might happen*, Dave wondered. *Probably not or they wouldn't be here.*

He went to the upper deck and looked down at the field where Washington was a bat. A costumed mascot was urging the crowd to cheer. He looked across the field to the centerfield gate and saw a crowd at the rail, smiling and cheering. The bullpens were quiet. It was too early for relievers to warm up, so they sat and glanced at the field and waited for the call.

This crowd would wait until the final out unless it was a blowout for Los Angeles. There would be a massive fireworks display after the game if Washington won and boaters were already on the Anacostia waiting for it. The team had done well and had led the league since the All Star break, but winning the division was a fight against Atlanta. For Los Angeles, the battle was against San Francisco. Both teams were exhausted from a long season and ready to move on. A lot was on the line. The fans were there to see and support the teams.

Dave looked down and experienced a moment of great affection for Washington as a city and as a team. The city took crap from all fifty states. The states sent their best and worst to Washington. *The problem isn't the city*, he thought. *It's the boobs who get sent here.*

There was a roar from the crowd as the ball sailed over the Washington bullpen and two runs scored. Everyone was on their feet as the Los Angeles pitcher stared at the batter smiling as he rounded the bases. High fives and back slaps in the Washington dugout.

He walked to the lower concourse and asked a security guard if he could go to the field level of the stadium, displaying his press pass. She waved him down and turned back to the game. He could not get past the guards at the locker rooms, so he watched as the photographers gathered in the tunnel that led to the field. He walked the bowels of the stadium and found himself at the loading dock where workers were smoking and waiting for the game to end so they could haul off trash and the spoils of the season that was ending.

A man in workman's clothing was crouched behind a van, staring into space. Dave thought he had seen the man before but no name came to him. The man was wearing a hat low over his face and glasses that made his eyes appear very large. Dave assumed the man had very bad eyesight and had a moment of pity for him. The man glanced at Dave and stood up. He removed his glasses and stared at Dave with a shock of recognition. He moved to the far side of the van against the fence and ran up the ramp and into the stadium.

No! Dave thought. *It can't be!* His heart pounded as he ran after Ghazali but the hallway was crowded and he lost him. "Stop that man!" he shouted to the confused people who looked from Dave to where he was pointing. Ghazali was not there and the crowd had no idea whether Dave was just drunk or trying to catch a friend.

He tried to call O'Neil but the cell phone signal in the lower level was weak. He ran back to the loading dock and where the signal was stronger and he pressed O'Neil's number on his phone.

The Inspector picked up on one ring. "Hello Scribe, how's the game?"

"I saw him. I saw this Ghazali guy. He was in the loading dock are. He ran into the stadium just now." Dave was breathless.

"How do you know it was him?"

"I've seen him before. I know it was him. He knows me, too. That's why he ran away. He's in the stadium right now."

"You stay where you are."

It took less than a minute for an agent to find Dave at the loading dock. Within five minutes a dozen agents were combing the immediate area and questioning everyone who had been there when Ghazali ran up the ramp and into the stadium. He was wearing green work clothes, they said, and a hat. His clothes were torn. He had a cut on his head. He was Mexican or something like that. He did not speak to anyone. He did not act in a way that made them suspicious. He came with another man and delivered something.

The answers were marginally helpful. He had cuts on his head and his clothes were torn. That narrowed the search. The word went out that the man they were looking for was in the stadium and was wearing torn green work clothes.

Fans going for beer or food saw frantic men and women running along the concourses, searching faces and examining clothing. Hispanic men were stopped and questioned. Vendors were searched again.

By the fifth inning break Gant decided to ask for help. A photo of Ghazali was displayed on the giant screen and the stadium announcer, in tones suitable for the introduction of a star batter, asked, "Have you seen this man? If you have, please contact the nearest police officer or security worker. Thank you." No explanation was given.

Ghazali missed the announcement. He was removing the costume of a team mascot who was slowly dying of a gunshot wound to his chest. Ghazali dragged the moaning man to isolated spot beneath a stairwell that was used mostly by the maintenance staff. He clubbed the man with the butt of his handgun and covered him with a cardboard box he had spread out. He placed the large, stuffed mascot head on his shoulders and ran onto the field to urge the fans to cheer for the home team.

Chapter Forty-Four

Dave called Sid at Now News and briefed him. He added, for the benefit of Gant's agents who might be listening, "Screw you, F.B.I."

"Get the hell out of there," Sid said. "I can't believe those sons of bitches aren't evacuating the stadium"

"They seem to think they can handle it," Dave said.

"Like the great job they're doing now," Sid said. Dave could hear Sid pounding his desk.

"This is going to end before eleven o'clock, one way or another. Keep the desk staffed and some editors around. Let's do a special report." Dave was wearing his reporter hat and was already writing the story.

"I'll send out an informal alert that a special report might be coming later tonight. No commitments. I'll call some of the major market station news directors and give them a heads up without offering any details. Hell, these folks would scoop us on our own story."

"Just for your information in case this goes south around here, this guy slipped through rings of security, killed his partner, and is now making Gant look like a fool. It's all tied to the electric grid outages and the explosion a few days ago downtown. Make sure you wrap it up on your end if I can't."

Sid exploded. "Goddam it! You get your ass out of there! Every damn time you get yourself involved with O'Neil or the feds you damn near get killed. This is a mother of a story Dave but it's not worth your life."

"Bye bye, Sid." Dave hung up. He made his way to a tunnel leading to the field and stood behind the fence to watch the groundskeepers replace the bases during a break between innings. The used bases are sold to fans who collect everything associated with the game. They leveled the infield where players had created divots with their cleats, new bases were inserted into slots, and the umpires returned to their spots.

Nothing appeared to be out of order. Fans were waving cash at the men and women hawking beer, water, hot dogs, and peanuts. Kids were consuming all the food their parents would buy. A few men near Dave appeared to be drunk and were dancing, embarrassing their wives who were telling them to sit down. Normal.

He made some notes about the crowd and the field to use as color in the long-form pieces he would file overnight. He turned to walk back into the tunnel when a mascot stepped in front of him, appearing to be focused on the crowd. The mascot turn to him bowed, making a show for the fans. The mascot grabbed Dave's notebook and threw it up into a group of fans who were hoping to catch a free t-shirt.

The mascot slapped Dave on the back and ran into the tunnel. Dave followed him, angry and demanding that the whoever was in the costume go into the crowd to retrieve his notebook. He chased the man down a passageway and into an alcove, where the man removed his costume's large head. Dave stared into the face of Ghazali, who was smiling and waving a handgun.

"You are a fool, Mr. Haggard," Ghazali said in a heavy Spanish accent. "It is possible to know too much. Have you heard that before. It is possible to know too much." He looked into Dave's eyes.

Dave hestitated. He didn't know whether to confront Ghazali or run for help. He turned his head to see if anyone was near who might come to his aid when the butt of the handgun smashed into the base of his skull. He saw a bright light, heard a crunch, and fell to the floor. Ghazali raised the gun to use it as a club to beat Dave's head until he was dead but a group of custodians walked toward them, clapping to the time of the stadium organ, which was trying to whip the fans into noisy support of the team.

Ghazali pulled Dave into the alcove, put on the mascot head, and ran back on to the field. Dave came around to the sound of cheering. He did not know where he was or why he was lying on concrete. His head hurt and pulsed and blood was caking on his eyes. He had trouble opening them. When he managed to pull his eyelids up he saw a cement wall a few inches from his face. He tried to sit up but his legs had grown numb and he had a moment of panic when he thought he was paralyzed. He tried to call out but his voice was weak against the crowd's cheering and the stadium organ.

He rubbed his legs and feeling slowly returned, allowing him to move them. He propped himself against the wall and waited for someone to help him, but no one paid attention to anything except what was happening on the field. The cheering went on for several minutes. A maintenance worker pushing a cargo cart rolled it toward the alcove and turned away toward the field as the cart stopped at the alcove, blocking Dave's view of the hallway. He leaned forward and tried to move it but he was too weak and blood was dripping into his eyes. He was lightheaded and dizzy and felt sick to his stomach. He knew these were signs of a concussion and told himself he must not fall asleep.

He regained enough feeling in his legs to roll onto his hands and knees and make his way to the cart. He tried to push it away from the alcove but it would not move. The front of the cart was pressing against the corner where the alcove and the wall met. He pushed it the other way and it moved an inch or two but the effort exhausted him.

The flat part of the cart where cargo was stacked was three feet off the floor. The sides were shelves where smaller items could be placed as they were delivered. The shelves prevented him from seeing to the other side of the cart or crawling under it. He sat and stared, taking deep breaths, as he fought off the urge to close his eyes and sleep. He pounded his fists against his chest and found energy to get up on his knees. He used his hands to slowly climb up the shelves on the cart and reach the flat portion where he pulled himself high enough to allow him to lie face. It was smooth and his hands slipped as he tried to get more of his body on to the cart. He fell back and lay on the alcove floor, staring up.

He lifted up on one elbow, turned onto his hands and knees, and tried again, this time pushing himself high enough to allow him to bend forward at the waist, with his upper body on the flat part of the cart. He pushed his arms out far enough to grab the far side, which allowed him to hold on.

"Help! Help!" he tried to shout but his voice was weak and drowned out by the noise coming from the stadium.

He leaned in the direction the cart would move and managed to scoot it a few inches before he was exhausted. He repeated this until he had no more energy and he stopped, defeated. He lay his head on the cart and stared down the hallway, waiting for an explosion or darkness to overcome him.

His mind was lost in a dream-like image of Elena at the beach in Ocean City. *I should have been nicer to you.* In the dream she was walking away from him as he shouted his apologies. *I am so sorry.*

He felt his body sliding over the cart and thought he was falling back into the alcove but he was moving in the wrong direction. He heard a voice, then another.

"Jesus! Dave, are you alright?" It was O'Neil and he was pulling Dave into the hallway. "Get help!"

Dave heard the other voice speak into a radio. "Yes, right now!" the voice said.

O'Neil's face appeared. "Can you talk? What happened?"

Dave thought it was another dream. "Elena. Get Elena back. I don't want to dream about you."

"Elena is not here, Dave. What happened?"

O'Neil lifted Dave's head and gave him some water from a plastic bottle. "Come on, Dave, talk to me."

"He came after me," Dave said.

"Who?"

"Ghazali. He's the mascot."

Agents were gathered around Dave. A paramedic arrived and pushed everyone away. O'Neil grabbed his radio. "Ghazali is wearing a mascot costume. He damn hear killed Dave."

"Roger that," Gant responded.

O'Neil motioned to the agents. "Follow me."

Forty-Five

Ghazali was in his own dream-like state, imagining that his forthcoming seventy-two virgins were even now looking down at him, smiling and awaiting his embrace. He had no doubt that he could perform to their satisfaction once earthly limitations were overcome through martyrdom. The mascot costume was stuffed into a dumpster and had been replaced by a security guard's uniform, the guard having been dispatched during the cheering for a ground-rule double. The guard was now under the mascot costume in the dumpster.

He wore sunglasses to cover his eyes and a security service baseball cap down low over his face. He walked upright in a get-out-of-my-way manner, causing those he passed to move over. He created the impression that he was on his way to something important which, to his mind, was true.

In his dazed state he had committed himself to carry out his mission during the fireworks that would follow a Washington victory, which Ghazali assumed was destined. He must wait for the end of the game to end everything else. He looked skyward and smiled at his virgins. *I am on my way. God is most Glorious. I am not a pagan.*

These people are pagans. He offered a smirk to the crowd. *It is they who must perish.*

He saw a group of F.B.I. agents gathered near a tunnel to the field. They appeared to be scanning the grounds and the stands. A costumed mascot was walking down the stairs in the first section along the first base line and the agents ran to the stairs and brought the mascot down, shouting and pulling the large head from a young man who was screaming. "What's happening? Who are you?"

The agents pulled the man to his feet and dragged him down the stairs to the field and into a tunnel that led to the bowels of the stadium. A few fans shouted "What's going on?" and the agents responded with "Nothing to worry about."

Ghazali laughed and imagined the fright the young man in the costume was experiencing. *Too bad for you.*

***

O'Neil was waiting for the agents to bring the young man to him. He knew immediately that the fellow as not Ghazali. "Have you been here for the entire game?" O'Neil asked.

"I got here at three o'clock, like always. What's this about?" The young man was a student at Georgetown who moonlighted as a costumed character at baseball games in the summer and kids' birthday parties during the off-season. He had never been arrested.

O'Neil pulled two photos from his inside pocket. "You ever see these men?" The photos were of Ghazali and Maskhadov.

"I don't know. You see a lot of guys who look like that around here."

"Look closely. Did you see either of these men here today?"

"I don't know. Maybe. Are they guards or something?"

"Easy question. Yes or no." O'Neil softened his voice.

"I really don't know." The young man looked frightened.

"How many people wear costumes during games?"

"Different numbers. Depends on the day. We have the guys in the President's costumes and the regular mascot plus other things sometimes. Depends."

"Anybody seem suspicious?" O'Neil was in full detective attitude.

"Here? No. Regular guys."

"Anybody missing right now?"

"We swap off sometimes, so guys come and go. I wouldn't know. I'm on the clock now, that's all I know."

"Here's what I need you to do. Ask around if anybody's seen these guys and if any of the mascot people are missing. If the answer is yes, find one of these agents and they will bring me to you or you to me. Got it?" O'Neil offered his hand.

The young man's blank face told O'Neil that the fellow was probably going to go home and tell his friends how the F.B.I. had tackled him during a game.

"Give your name and address to the agents. We may need to contact you. Do not say anything about our conversation unless and until I say it's okay. Got it?"

"Okay. May I leave?"

"Off you go." O'Neil offered an arm sweep to send the young man on his way. He waited until the fellow was out of earshot and told an agent to gather everyone in costume and bring them to him.

Thirty minutes later O'Neil learned that a man named Darnell Turner was missing. He had been assigned to wear a mascot costume for the first five innings and then take a break. Fifteen minutes later an agent reported that Turner's body was found under some cardboard under a stairwell. Shortly after that another body was found in a dumpster along with Turner's costume.

"Three bodies and we're not at the seventh's inning stretch," O'Neil said. "Hell of a game we have going here. Maybe Ghazali wants to pick us off one at a time. At this rate it will take him days."

"Not funny," Gant said. "Get back to the trailer and we can regroup."

"We do a lot of that," O'Neil said.

"It only matters at the end, Inspector."

"You know he's thinking that, too."

"To hell with him." Gant yelled into the radio. O'Neil wondered if she was losing it.

Chapter Forty-Six

A team of C.I.A. agents was parked in a van on South Capitol Street, listening to the communication between Gant, O'Neil and the agents. At Langley, another team was listening as two psychologists trained to interpret human speech patterns took notes and offered analysis of the state of mind of everyone on the F.B.I. network at the stadium.

"This is a situation on the edge," offered one of them.

"No one is running this operation," said the other.

The Director was sitting in a leather chair with his eyes closed. He had not spoken in the two hours the monitors had been active. He stood up. "Here's what I need to know. Is this guy Ghazali going to blow up the stadium? Can the F.B.I. stop it? Tell me what's wrong with how this is being handled."

"Gant is taking the riskiest approach," said one of the psychologists. "She's betting she can nail this guy before he pulls the trigger. She's on edge. She knows it could go south. I don't understand her reasoning."

"How would we handle it?" the Director said.

"We would have taken out Ghazali and Maskhadov before they got within a thousand yards of the stadium." The speaker was a leader of an anti-terrorist unit known for preemptive assassinations and kidnappings.

"So here's the big question," the Director said. "Who's running Ghazali and Maskhadov? Al Qaeda? ISIS? Some new nutcase in Pakistan? Even if Gant's team stops this thing it's not over. Whoever sent these guys here will send more. Hell, Americans are joining these groups and the next ones who turn up with bombs might look just like everybody else around here."

"With all due respect, what does everybody else here look like?" The anti-terrorist unit leader had raised his hand. "This is Washington. Black, brown, yellow, red, and even white people are everybody. If we were in Kansas we might have a shot at picking somebody out of a crowd but we're not. Appearance doesn't matter."

"You're missing my point," the Director said. "They'll keep coming unless we cut off the head. Intel lost this chase because we lost the targets. Now the F.B.I. is in position to either be the heroes and be carried around on the shoulders of the media or be the goats to be slaughtered if it all goes boom at the stadium. This is a crummy position to be in. Not only for us but for the country. You all with me?"

Heads nodded. The Director sat in his chair and silently stared at the monitoring equipment. "See if we can get some agents into the stadium. Our guys are better than the F.B.I.'s. Maybe we can bring this to an end."

***

Gant sat in her trailer and listened as one of her agents told her the operation was under surveillance. "My guess is it's C.I.A. keeping an eye on us," he said.

"Damn. Am I supposed to divert resources so we can keep an eye on them keeping an eye on us? I don't suppose any D.E.A. or military types are around."

"Congressman Taylor is plugged into the military, so maybe he has some friends in the neighborhood," the agent said.

"Great. What are they here as, action heroes?"

There was a knock on the door. Gant stared at it and waited. Another knock. "What the hell?" she said. "Whoever it is tell them the bathroom is in the stadium."

An agent opened the door and saw two men in suits and sunglasses. "Hello. Is Special Agent Gant available?" one of them said.

"Ask who it is?" Gant replied.

"We're from Langley," said the man.

"Ah, Jesus! Come on in." Gant stood up and glared at the two men stepping inside. "To what do I owe this honor?"

"We've been sent to offer assistance, Ma'am."

"By whom?"

"By the Director."

"And why would the Director even know where I am, much less feel a need to come to my aid?"

"Above my pay grade, ma'am." Both spooks removed their sunglasses to reveal neutral facial expressions and eyes that offered no clues.

"Well, I suppose we could use some coffee," Gant said.

"I believe our help would be of a more positive kind," the man said.

"What's your name?"

"I am Mister Jones and this is Mister Smith. We have colleagues who are nearby and ready to help."

"May I ask what sort of help you think you can provide?" Gant's voice was weary.

"After you brief us we will have some suggestions."

"I have no intention of briefing you. I assume you need no briefing given that you barged in here ready to save the day. You may tell your superiors that you offered and we passed. Now you can go back to your little van and watch us do our work."

"You don't have much time," Mister Smith said. "We are here to help."

"How would you know how much time we have?" Gant said.

"This is not a secret operation, ma'am. The intel community is small."

"So what do you think is going to happen?"

"We believe there is a short window before this ends. We know you lost Ghazali more times than you had him. We know Ghazali killed Maskhadov. We know he attacked the journalist Dave Haggard. We know he had and discarded a mascot costume and is now at large prepared to carry out his mission." Mister Smith had no expression as he recited his facts.

"What else?" Gant was interested.

"You need help."

"Can you work with us or are you trying to run this operation?"

"You tell us."

"Go to the stadium and find Inspector O'Neil. Tell him I sent you, then tell him what you told me. Let's see if you're as good as you say you are."

Forty-Seven

Dave's head hurt but the E.M.S. technician had stopped the bleeding. He was dizzy but he could stand. He was in a small medical office where a doctor was asking him questions and instructing him to touch his nose and stand on one foot, the kind of thing a cop asks suspected drunk drivers to do. He was a bit wobbly but coming around.

"You'll be fine," the doctor said. "Take it easy for a day or two and take pain relievers as needed. Drink plenty of liquids and stay away from alcohol. I wouldn't take part in sports for a week or so."

O'Neil stood back and reviewed his notes. One of Gant's agents was at the door. The radio earbud came to life in O'Neil's left ear. "Inspector, a couple of spooks are on their way to offer help. Listen to what they say and go with your instincts." Gant's voice was tinny and stressed.

"Roger that," O'Neil said. The agent at the door had heard the same message and raised his eyebrows.

"You up to this or do you want to leave?" O'Neil said.

"If you're in, I'm in," Dave said, looking pale.

"Why don't you drink some juice or something," O'Neil said.

"That's when you give blood," Dave said.

"You gave blood all over the floor," O'Neil said, holding the door open.

"Screw you," Dave said. He wore a bandage on his head and he limped from a bruised hip. He had the look of a man who had either been hit by a bus or lost a round in a heavyweight bout. He was thirsty and angry. "I don't know about cops, but reporters sometimes wonder what the hell they were thinking when they went into the business."

"Every day," O'Neil said. "It was either be a cop or a bank robber and I'm not good at holdup notes."

***

Misters Smith and Jones found O'Neil on the upper concourse eating area, where he, Dave and an agent were pouring over a map of the stadium, circling places that were out of the way and likely hiding spots for someone on the run. It was the tenth time they had gone over the map and nothing new had come to them.

Smith and Jones stood quietly while the men at the table looked stumped. Smith cleared his throat and waited for O'Neil to look up. O'Neil knew who they were and made a show of making them wait for a response. He turned the map this way and that, upside down and sideways, and looked up at Smith. "I hear you guys are going to save the day."

"We're only here to help," Smith said. Jones had not said a word to either Gant or O'Neil.

"So I gather. So, Chief, what's the plan?"

Smith went through the line he had given Gant, explaining what was known about the Gant operation and the situation in the stadium. His voice was flat and without judgement. He finished and stood silently.

"And?" O'Neil said.

"What can we do for you?" Smith said.

"Look, we appreciate your offer but unless you guys know more than we do, we've got this."

"It doesn't appear that you do, given that this fellow Ghazali is here somewhere getting ready to blow the place up. And these fine folks in the stands are here because they believe they and their families are safe." Smith held a steady gaze at O'Neil.

"And your assertion is that had you guys been running this Ghazali would be neutralized and this operation would be over." O'Neil had a bite to his voice.

"We're only here to help," Smith said.

"Have a seat," O'Neil said, pointing to a nearby table. Smith and Jones sat down and leaned toward O'Neil. "Ideas?"

"I take it clearing the stadium is out of the question," Smith said.

"For now, yes," O'Neil said. "I have no opinion at this point."

Smith turned to Dave. "Did you get a good look at him."

"Twice," Dave said. "The first time he ran and the second time he knocked me out."

"You're lucky," Smith said. "He killed the others."

"If you say so," Dave said. To Dave, Smith was smug and smelled of arrogance.

"So," O'Neil said, "What's your plan?"

"Smoke him out. Make him come to us," Smith said.

"We tried that. Even put his picture up on the big screen. Nothing. He's disciplined and knows what he's doing."

"What about a pony show, lots of law enforcement running around making noise?" Smith waited for an answer.

"What do we tell the good folks in the stands eating hog dogs and buying their kids expensive souvenirs? That we're using the game as a backdrop for a training exercise?"

"Don't tell them anything." Jones spoke for the first time.

O'Neil looked at both C.I.A. men. "Aren't you guys supposed to be good at secret operations? I don't see how a police pony show is secret."

"We are good at other things," Jones said.

"Like what?" O'Neil was showing his impatience.

"We get things done." Jones had the look of a man who thought he had scored a point.

"Yeah, well, get back to me on that." O'Neil looked at Dave. "Are you getting this??

Smith leaned in and glared at O'Neil. "None of this is on the record and if Dave makes any of it public he will be charged under U.S. Code 798 - Disclosure of classified information and, yes, he will go to prison."

"Are you a real agent or just a dipshit who makes threats?" O'Neil's face was red.

"Are you going to work with us or not?" Smith and Jones stood.

"Tell you what. Go to the centerfield gate and watch who comes and goes. If Ghazali shows up, call me." O'Neil turned his back on the C.I.A. men and waited for them to leave. The F.B.I. agent sitting at the table with him nodded when the C.I.A. men were gone. O'Neil spoke into the radio microphone protruding from his cuff. "Our friends are leaving."

Gant responded in seconds. "On their own?"

"Kind of."

"Get back to the trailer. We need to sort this out."

***

The Director and other C.I.A. types listened and shook their heads. "After 9/11 we were all supposed to make nice. We'll have to do this on our own." He turned to an aide. "Tell them to move."

The men in the van emerged wearing shorts, baseball hats and team jerseys. They looked like the fans in the stadium, which was the idea. They entered through different gates using valid tickets.

Chapter Forty-Eight

Ghazali was sitting on the second level in a seat that had been empty for most of the game. He had scouted such seats, knowing that some fans with tickets fail to show up, even at big games. He was wearing clothing taken from a man who was careless enough to look for an out-of-the-way place to sneak a cigarette. Smoking is banned in the stadium and smokers have long sought ways to light up during games. Security people who follow the smell of tobacco smoke either scold or eject the miscreants. The poor fellow Ghazali encountered had the misfortune of lighting up during a game in which security personnel were occupied with other things. The man's body was stuffed into a garbage can on the lower level in an area where vendors stored trash to be picked up after games.

He sat in his seat wearing shorts, a team shirt, a team hat and sandals that upon close examination were two sizes too big. No one was looking at his feet. No one was looking at him at all. The game was tied. The stadium announcer was urging everyone to stand and make noise. The organ was pumping up the energy.

He stood with the fans around him, clapping and smiling. He did not wave his hat with the others. He wore the reading glasses that made his eyes look large and changed the appearance of his face. He smiled and nodded to those around him, speaking in Spanish. "Es un gran juego! Podemos ganar." *It is a great game. We can win.*

A woman next to him smiled and nodded, not understanding what he was saying. She was with two children and a man Ghazali assumed was her husband. They were blond and appeared to be comfortably middle class. He believed that people like this family were responsible for the pain and suffering of the world's poor and he had no remorse about what he was about to do. He smiled and turned back to the field.

***

In the press box Charlie Steiner was telling listeners in Southern California that the score was tied going in to the bottom of the sixth inning. There was a commercial break and he took the time to run to the men's room. Years on the air had trained him to address his needs in less than two minutes, including travel time. He stood and looked down at the stands and saw a group of men running to several sections, using small binoculars to scan the crowd. He tapped a fellow broadcaster from Los Angeles. "Something's up. Keep an eye out for me. Be right back."

The game resumed and the men with binoculars moved from section to section, scanning the fans in the seats and pointing out those who were dark-skinned, male, and thin. Other men ran to those who had been singled out and escorted them to the mezzanine, where they were photographed and questioned. All of the men were allowed to return to their seats. No explanation was offered.

The woman sitting next to Ghazali saw what was happening and asked no one in particular, "What's going on? What are those men doing?"

Ghazali knew what was going on. They were looking for him. He glanced up the stairs to the concourse and saw nothing unusual but he gauged that those with the binoculars would soon spot him. He pulled his hat low and told the woman next to him that he was going for a beer and would be right back. She paid no attention to him.

He climbed to the concourse and stood next to an usher. "Great game," he said in English.

"Yeah, we got a shot," the usher said, not looking at him.

"I think I'm gonna get sick. Maybe something I ate. Where can I go?" Ghazali said.

The usher turned to look at him. "Not here. Try the men's room." He turned back to the field.

Ghazali found an elevator and pressed "DOWN." He waited while it came to the concourse and rode it to the ground level. He found a hallway with rooms on either side and told a security guard that an usher told him there was a medical office on that level and he needed help.

"Upper level," She said. "You can ride up with me."

"I need to rest for a minute," he said.

She then got into the elevator, glanced at him, and the door closed.

He ran from door to door hoping to find one that was unlocked and unoccupied. He found a closet where cleaning supplies were stored and climbed over a bucket to a back rack where he could hide behind a stack of boxes. He turned out the light and sat down. He chuckled to himself as he fondled the detonator. *I could do it right now. I will wait for the fireworks.*

***

The C.I.A. men pulled two dozen dark skinned men from their seats and questioned them. All were released. It was no surprise to the Director. He did not expect to find Ghazali out in the open casually enjoying the ball game. He wanted him to know that he was being hunted by people who were doing more than standing around. He wanted him to feel fear. The Director had no way of knowing that at that moment his prey was beyond fear. He was consumed by exuberation and a longing to see and be with his promised virgins. Death was to be welcomed, not feared. The Director told his agents to keep looking.

***

O'Neil and the F.B.I. agents assigned to him were scouring the dark under-the-stairs spots and odd angles in the stadium where things could be hidden. Bodies had already been found and O'Neil believed more were to be discovered. "We're dealing with a really sick individual," he said.

"You seem to attract these guys," Dave said.

"You, too. I seem to recall a certain priest killer who nearly killed you and your girlfriend and a professional hit man who shot you down."

"Another reason for me to find another line of work," Dave said.

"What? And give up show business?" O'Neil laughed at this old chestnut of a joke.

The seventh-inning stretch began with the singing of America the Beautiful. The crowd was patriotic and joined in with feeling, causing Dave stop and sing along. His eyes teared as he gazed at the crowd singing and holding hands over their hearts, facing the American flag. *These are good people*, he thought. *These are my people.* He felt a moment of immense pride. A moment later the crowd burst into Take Me Out to the Ballgame and the mood changed to happiness and a feeling of sharing this moment with forty thousand others.

"Baseball is a great game," Dave said.

"Damn right," O'Neil said. "It makes football look crude."

"Remind me of that in November," Dave said.

Chapter Forty-Nine

The Director was wearing his usual scowl, a Winston Churchill-like expression that his aides had come to see as his real face. He was never happy, at least in the opinion of his staff. He was privy to information that would keep most people up nights under their beds. His view of humanity was shaped by the evil he knew was waiting to claim all that he held dear. He was not a man who worried about the niceties of the "open world" as he referred to all that was public. It was all public relations, in his view, and had no more connection to reality than the Saturday morning cartoons. There was what you said and there was what you did. Only what you did mattered.

He sat behind his large desk and made a tent out of his fingers. "Are you familiar with the term 'military grade technology?'"

A few heads nodded. The Director scowled at them. "There are things we can do that we never talk about in public. There was a vague reference a few years back in the Washington Post about some of it but we managed to get it back in the bottle. There are two reasons we don't talk about it, even at the White House and certainly not to Congress. One is nobody there can keep his or her mouth shut and two is we don't want the bad guys to know what we have. If they know, they'll want it as well."

"Yes, Sir," an aide said, nodding his head.

"Don't be a toady, Cy. Just listen." The Director glared at Cy, a mid-level deputy director.

"Yes, Sir," Cy said, drawing smirks from the others.

"One of these military grade technical capabilities allows us to gather real time DNA by pointing a device at a crowd, scanning the crowd, and waiting for a match that has been programmed into the device. It's been used in Iraq and Afghanistan and is now being used on certain sensitive missions around the world. It allows us to find and apprehend individuals who previously would have evaded us. If we can seize them before they can hide among civilians we can save lives. It's that simple."

Nods all around.

"These devices are closely kept and are used only with very high authorization. Very high. Do I make myself clear?"

Again, nods.

"Which brings me to the current situation at Nationals Park. It's obvious that the F.B.I. is unable to get a handle on this. There's a Keystone Cops aspect to this. Ghazali gets nabbed, released, lost, found, lost, found again, murders people, and does everything except wave his dick at the agents who are trying to follow him. We've been turned away. But right now we have a pretty obvious operation going on there but it's just to show the flag. This thing could blow anytime."

"What's the play?" A field agent named Stein raised his hand.

"Glad you asked," the Director said. "The aforementioned device is now at the stadium and the crowd is being scanned. When we get a match on DNA for this fellow Ghazali we'll take him out, due process be damned."

Those gathered in the Director's office applauded and high-fived each other. The Director raised his hands. "This is not a basketball game. Be professional."

***

One of the Director's teams knocked on Gant's trailer door and requested a meeting. This was a diversion to grab her attention while another team scoured the stadium with a device that looked like an electronic rifle. The device was disguised as a long microphone for a satellite radio station. The team was dressed in matching electric green t-shirts and the agents held up signs reading, "Say Hello to America! Be on Worldwide Radio." The device was pointed at fans and the agents yelled, "Say hello to America!" The fans were happy to join in and within minutes sections of the stadium erupted in shouts "Hello America!" accompanied by smiling and waving, even though no mention of video had been made.

The device transmitted information to a computer station in a van where DNA from the shouting fans was processed that commercial computer makes could only dream about. By the bottom of the eighth inning thousands of samples had been taken but there were no matches.

The Director sat in his office and followed the team in real time. "In Afghanistan these things are used at choke points, so it's not as random and scattered. We'll keep looking."

In her trailer Gant was growing irritated with the C.I.A. team that had become comfortable occupying space. One of the agents was very friendly and tried to bond with her, which she recognized as a tactic to keep her at ease. She went over what the team had said and realized that it was meaningless pap designed to sound like operational conversation. She was being played. The C.I.A. was running an operation in the stadium.

She interrupted what one of the agents was saying and slammed her fist down on her desk. She stood up and pointed to the door. "Get out! Get the hell out."

The C.I.A. men smiled, stood, and silently left the trailer.

She used the radio to contact O'Neil. "They've got something going on in the stadium. I'll be right there."

Chapter Fifty

Ghazali woke from his dreamlike state when he heard the stadium announcer say that the ninth inning had begun and it was time to make some noise. He felt weary. He knew his energy was leaving him. He felt fear. It was time.

He knelt on the concrete floor and hoped he was facing the Holy City of Mecca. He recited his prayer of death with a passage from the Qur'an.

Proclaim: "O My servants who exceeded the limits, never despair of God's mercy. For God forgives all sins. He is the Forgiver, Most Merciful."

It did not occur to Ghazali that he was not a forgiver of those who had offended him or Him. He wept as he stood, holding the detonator as though it were a holy object. He held it up.

With the Name of Allah, Allah is the Most Great! O Allah, accept it from me.

He placed the detonator in his pocket and looked to see if anyone was nearby. He was alone in a remote spot at the bottom of the stadium. He had triumphed. He placed the baseball cap on his head and the glasses on his face. His vision was blurred by the thick lenses but he could see well enough to make his way to an elevator. He got off on the main concourse and walked through a crowd of fans who were preparing to leave when the game ended.

A group of men in loud green shirts was making noise and pointing something at the fans, who were shouting Hello! Everyone was having a good time. He had no cheer to share. The men with the device pointed it at him and shouted "Say hello to America." He kept walking, head down, and brushed against one of the men. The man stared at Ghazali and motioned for the men with him to come to him.

Ghazali ran through the crowd shouting, "Those men are trying to rob me!" Some of the men in the crowd stepped in front of the men in the green t-shirts, blocking them from chasing Ghazali. He hid behind a portable beer cart to catch his breath while the men in the green t-shirts fanned out. He broke through a small knot of teenagers who were laughing at a joke one of them had told. He pushed a girl aside to get through the group as the girl raised her voice at him. "So rude. You're like, so rude." She turned back to her friends as the men in the green t-shirts brushed them aside.

Ghazali fled into an alcove that overlooked the field and slipped to the side where fans in wheelchairs were sitting in a space that had been set aside for them. He pushed past the wheelchairs and found a group of men who were standing and watching the game. He turned his hat around and stood with his back to the men in the green shirts, who glanced down the space where he had been and moved on.

He made his way to an area where young men and women were drinking beer, making out, and watching the action on the field. In the press box Charlie Steiner was telling listeners in California that the score was tied at five going into the bottom of the ninth inning. Washington would win the game by scoring. Ghazali began to breathe hard and he felt light-headed. It was dark and skies were clear. A single run would mean victory for Washington and the fireworks would begin.

He looked at those around him and wondered if the blast would bring down the area where he was standing. He was overlooking centerfield. Before him was a packed stadium where thousands of men, women and children were standing and cheering. He allowed himself to believe they were cheering for him, the great martyr, he alone who had the courage to do this deed.

Chapter Fifty-One

Gant and her agents stormed through the centerfield gate and turned to follow the concourse's third base line to a knot of men in green t-shirts. She confronted the men and grabbed the rifle-like device they were waving at the fans.

"I told you I don't need your help. What the hell do you think you're doing?" She leaned into the face of the man holding the device.

"We are on assignment," the man said.

"To do what?"

"We are only here to help," the man said.

"I've heard that before and it scares me. When someone says they're here to help it really means they're here to screw me." Gant walked away, motioning for O'Neil and her agents to follow. Dave was still woozy and stopped to catch his breath. He didn't have the energy to follow them. He was thirsty. He saw a vendor stand to his left and went to buy a bottle of water. He drank deeply and walked to the rail overlooking centerfield. Young people were drinking beer and watching the game and each other. Dave was twenty feet from Ghazali but did not look in his direction.

Ghazali was watching the game as Washington's star leftfielder came to the plate. He did not look around, confident that he was safe in the small crowd of young drinkers. The first pitch was low and outside. A ball. The next pitch was a sinker and a called strike. One and one. The next pitch was high and inside. Ball two. Then a fastball. Swing and a miss. Two and two. Ghazali raised up on his toes to get a better view of the scoreboard where the fireworks would explode should Washington score. The people around him were shouting and clapping their hands.

Dave leaned against the rail, watching the pitcher. He felt better. His head was clearing. Ball three. Full count. *This is as good as it gets*, he thought. *It's all on the line.* The pitcher went through his pre-throw motions, removing his hat and wiping his brow, stomping around the mount and looking up at the sky. He stepped up to the rubber, planted his left foot, and fired a ninety-eight mile an hour fastball at the plate. The sound of the bat making contact made it all the way to the people standing next to Dave. The ball rose into the lights and some in the crowd groaned that it did not have the distance to make it over the outfield fence. The ball went over the heads of the Los Angeles outfielders who were running and following its flight.

The ball moved right to left from home plate to centerfield and Dave's gaze followed it as it sank into the stands that overlooked the gap between left field and centerfield. A cheer rose up as the crowd celebrated. He looked at the people near him and saw a face that made him freeze. There, barely out of reach, was Ghazali, laughing and holding up something that looked like a strange flashlight. Ghazali was watching the scoreboard.

Dave experienced a surge, a rage, and pushed the other fans aside as he rushed toward Ghazali, who was unaware that Dave was there. Dave's forward motion propelled him through a small group of fans who were jumping up and down and spilling beer on themselves and others. He did not stop to confront Ghazali. He ran into him and began to pummel him with his fists. He had read somewhere that the most sensitive part of a man is his testicles, so he pounded Ghazali's, producing howling screams that quieted the crowd nearby.

Ghazali held the detonator up and raised his thumb to the button on top. Dave realized that he was looking at the trigger of a conflagration. He grabbed Ghazali's wrist and bent it backward in an attempt to wrestle the detonator out of the terrorists hand. He was losing his energy. The adrenaline that had helped him attack Ghazali was dissipating. He was losing.

Ghazali sensed that Dave's grip was weakening and all he needed to do was let it play out. He relaxed and a smile returned to his face. He used his left hand as a claw to attack Dave's face and divert his attention from the detonator. Dave screamed as Ghazali's fingers pressed into his eyes.

He pressed his weight against Ghazali's right arm, hoping to press it to the concrete surface of the concourse. He felt Ghazali's strength returning and his own ebbing away. "Help me!" he shouted.

In the noise of the celebration and the fireworks that were now filling the skies over the stadium, Dave's cry for help was unheard. He prepared for the worst. He braced himself for the explosions that would bring down the stadium or, in the best case, only part of it.

Ghazali went limp. His hand dropped from Dave's face. Dave looked down at Ghazali and saw that part of his head was gone, replaced by bloody mess of bone and gray pulp. He looked up into the faces of O'Neil and Gant. Both of their weapons were drawn and whisps of smoke were drifting from the barrels.

"You okay?" O'Neil asked.

Dave fainted.

Afterward

The official investigation blamed what the bureaucrats called "systemic deficiencies" for the near-disaster that night. A panel of former members of Congress, a retired federal judge, a former Director of the F.B.I. and a former Director of the C.I.A. listened to testimony, reviewed official records, and conducted closed-door hearings. In the peculiar language of these inquiries, it was stated that there was "no one, single cause" of the near-miss.

Patricia Gant was mentioned as a "strong leader whose bravery is without question." Inspector O'Neil was cited for his "determination and commitment to public safety." Each was given a new assignment that, according to the report, "represented a significant increase in responsibility and authority." Both assignments were to panels whose missions were "oversight and monitoring," meaning yet another dead-end job that, the panel hoped, would cause both Gant and O'Neil to vanish from all official radar.

The Director of the C.I.A. informed the panel that a group known as The Knife was responsible for the attempt to blow up the stadium. It had been based in Pakistan but had moved its operation to Syria where it was engaged in bitter combat with various extremist groups trying to gain control of portions of a troubled region. There was no evidence that The Knife had further plans to attack the United States.

The investigating panel had its harshest words for Dave Haggard, accusing him of "irresponsible self-promotion at the expense of public safety and order." His primary sin had been in reporting details of how the operation to stop Markhadov and Ghazali had unraveled at every step. His statement that Ghazali had come "within half an inch" of blowing up Nationals Park was described as "irresponsible and without merit."

The news community had another reaction. Dave won a Peabody and DuPont/Columbia, along with other national and regional awards. He was feted at media dinners and was asked to be a paid speaker at conventions and business meetings.

Dave asked Sid to take him off the Justice Department beat because he was no longer welcome at the Attorney General's news conferences and was removed from the Department's press release list.

Sid refused. "If they don't like you it means you're doing your job."

~*~*~

Meet our Author

Larry Matthews

Larry Matthews is a former broadcast journalist in Washington whose awards include a George Foster Peabody Award for Excellence in Broadcasting, a DuPont/Columbia Citation, a National Headliner Award and many other national and regional awards for journalism.

Previous Dave Haggard Thrillers:
        Butterfly Knife
        Brass Knuckles

Other books by Larry Matthews

Take a Rifle from a Dead Man
Healing Charles
Saving Charles
I Used To Be In Radio
Street Business (with Ernie Lijoi Sr)
Unsung Heroes of the Old Line State

Watch for the next Dave Haggard thriller in 2015.

Nine-Millimeter Afternoon

A tale of lust and betrayal at the highest levels of power.

Dave Haggard is drawn into a web of erotic deceit as he investigates a lead linking powerful Washington figures to a trafficking ring that provides the nation's leaders with depraved amusement. The story takes him from the multi-million dollar mansions of the rich and powerful to the barred cages where innocents are groomed to be the slaves of decadence.